HOLY
MASQUERADE

Beyond all masks.
Beyond the death mask itself . . . .

After you have sensed the vertigo
And all the transformations:
The thumbscrew
And the revolving stage
And the emptiness that rests over the holy
And nothing, nothing more
comes
Out of the four gates —
Then comes the fifth corner of the world
And the year of the unicorn.

— BERTIL MALMBERG

HOLY MASQUERADE

by
Olov Hartman

translated by
Karl A. Olsson

WILLIAM B. EERDMANS PUBLISHING COMPANY
GRAND RAPIDS, MICHIGAN

Originally published as *Helig Maskerad,* copyright © 1950 by Norlin Förlag AB,
Stockholm, Sweden. This English translation by Karl A. Olsson has been approved
by the author and is published by permission of Norlin Förlag.

Some of the materials in the notes on the chapter headings were drawn, with
permission, from *The Christian Year* by Edward T. Horn, III (pp. 100-12), copyright © 1957 by Muhlenberg Press, Philadelphia.

Printed in the United States of America
Reprinted 1991

Library of Congress Cataloging-in-Publication Data

Hartman, Olov.
   [Helig maskerad. English]
   Holy masquerade / by Olov Hartman; translated by Karl A. Olsson.
     p.   cm.
   Translation of: Helig maskerad.
   ISBN 0-8028-6006-0
   I. Title.
PT9876.18.A7H4513   1991
839.73′74 — dc20   91-19089
                                               CIP

Contents

1

Esto Mihi: Be thou for Me*

I SHALL FOLLOW HIM. THAT IS THE SOLUTION. THIS IS THE third time I have sat in church on a Sunday in Lent, and, while Albert has expounded the text about following the Master on the way of sorrows, have looked as attentive and as pious as is proper for the wife of a minister. No, I have no intention to follow Jesus. I want to continue to follow my common sense. I want to continue to be as honest as possible. What I am now doing is a kind of self-defense. I want to save myself from the pious roles imposed on me. I want to save

* The author frequently uses words from medieval Latin liturgies as chapter headings. These headings have been retained in the English translation because of their close relevance to the respective chapters. All of them are derived from Scripture and are to be seen as keys to the development of Fru Klara Svensson's faith. *Esto mihi* are the first words of the introit for Quinquagesima Sunday, which is fifty days before Easter, and the Sunday before Ash Wednesday. The words are taken from Psalm 31:2 and mean "be thou for me." The entire phrase is translated in the RSV, "Be thou a rock of refuge for me, a strong fortress to save me." —Tr.

7

my true self from this life of sewing societies and church attendance. From this life of "May God's will be done." I want to dust my self off and give it back the clean colors it used to have. For that reason, old Klara — "the old man" as the provost says — is going to write these notations and follow Albert while he follows the Master on the way of sorrows. That will be delightful for the pre-Christian Klara, glitteringly delightful.

There is no question that this self has been in danger. First, by falling in love with a clergyman. I wonder many times how it happened. For the two of us lived in different worlds, or at least should have lived in two different worlds. But he was vicar in a city parish then and could present himself as a modern and free clergyman without risk to his popularity. He talked about spring on Easter Sunday and about the longing for eternity on Ascension Day. He played bridge and discussed the theater like an ordinary person. He represented a Christianity of a type which — well, it reminds me that at my confirmation someone gave me the poems of Fröding. Everything beautiful and pathetic by prophets and heretics was mixed together in a single soup, and I imagined that he and I could really meet one another in this religious confusion.

Furthermore he is a man; a rather handsome and pleasant person with blue eyes and curly blond hair and all that can intrigue a woman. You don't lose your sex even in a pew, and I am sure that I thought he preached adorably even when I did not think about the contents of what he said.

And when he began to show interest in me it wasn't long until I lost my reservations. The thought of a rural vicarage idyll did not seem very frightening at that time. What did I know of the imprisonment that awaits the worldly woman in the fragrance of coffee and lilacs in a country parsonage?

I was also reassured by the fact that Albert loved me in precisely the same way as a worldling. We had not known each other very long before he seduced me — passionately and competently. I thought: whatever you are in the pulpit, in the bedroom you will be a pagan. And it is yourself — the man without the cassock and without his Sunday-school button — it is the pagan I am marrying. I did not then suspect that he was capable of holding the kind of lecture on morality that he held before the youth of the parish the first summer we were here. He quoted the words of Paul frenetically: "Flee the fleshly lusts of youth." He warned against anticipating the rights of marriage and blew the battle trumpet against all that binds us to the earthly and all that sullies our purity. This did not hinder him from taking me the same night and from enjoying me in a very sophisticated way. Of course, we were married, but I think he would have done the same thing even if we had not been man and wife. In this respect he has not become very different from the first night we were together. He has not been any more released from the "animal."

Since we came to this parish, he has adopted a number of stereotypes that have no correspondence with reality. Much that he says and does is like a kaleidoscope. He mirrors himself in the pious opinion of good people and conforms himself to their ideal of a minister. I wonder if this doubleness, this theatrical religiosity, was not there from the beginning. I mean, from our beginning. For I notice, as I said a while ago, that the hypocritical spirit has gripped me as well. And this must have begun when we started to spin together the Christian and the secular. Although for him it was probably an old story. This does not concern me. I never asked him how it felt for him to give a clerical vow. I saw the formulary of ordination not so long ago and I thought that perhaps an honest person would have some difficulties with it. I mean an honest person in Albert's predicament. But, as I said, this does not concern me.

What does concern me, on the other hand, is my own ordination to the call of a pastor's wife. Why isn't there a special kind of marriage ceremony for clerical brides? That business about ministers not being offensive to anyone ought to be included in that ritual, together with a whole lot of other frightening things. For we wives of pastors are bound by the whole apparatus of piety. Perhaps we are bound even more than our husbands, for a minister receives some indulgences. But for a minister's wife, nothing is forgiven either in this world or in the world to come.

It can also be entered on my account that I agreed to a church wedding. Perhaps we can say that the values the bridal crown once represented have been inflated. With the arrival of birth control one can no longer determine the chastity of church brides, and the old tradition has little meaning. What is so repulsive is that the new morality is dignified by the old morality's symbols. And no one notices the contradiction. Albert and I should really have been married in a civil ceremony with a dance afterwards — a pagan dance in all honesty.

A part of me shivers when I write this way. This is a sign that I am on the right way. I shall walk that way until the end. So far the poison has not reached my heart. These notations will prove it.

No matter what Albert says, I shall rise out of my outer degradation. Tomorrow I shall go to the sewing society in war paint. I remember how Albert stopped me and took the lipstick away from me the first morning we came to the parish. "You can't go to the sewing society with red lips," he said. "You have to remember that you are a minister's wife, or you will be brought under judgment." I yielded — of course. The ministers call that *adiaphora;* it is supposed to mean "indifferent things." But how indifferent they are would soon appear if I permitted myself to dance at a wedding in the area, or if we served wine to the church council. *Adiaphora* are the things that the old women in the parish determine. It is enslavement unto death to pious tradition.

If we had some children, the whole thing would not have become so unbearable. Then I could have stayed home from a great deal. I could have blamed it on the difficulty of getting a babysitter. Then I should have been something more than just a minister's wife. There are not so many *adiaphora* in a mother's responsibilities. There is no difference between godly diapers and ungodly ones. In parsonages as well as in other homes you powder the bottoms of the children; in a parsonage the baby can bite a nipple just as sensually as elsewhere. If we had children I should have been able to control that part of my life without restriction and without hypocrisy. But now there are only Albert and myself, and our entire relationship is a problem of the minister and the minister's wife. Not even the most intimate part of our life escapes. I feel that it is being watched in some way. Some of the people in the parish wonder why we don't have any children — I feel this keenly. If one of the old ladies in the parish saw us, she would ask if what we did conformed with the scriptural injunction that one should "hold one's wife in honor and sanctity and not in the desire of the flesh"? If we got tired of one another and wanted to be divorced, it would be a scandal. Sometimes I seem to see a face in the bedroom window. A black and evil face. This is, of course, my nerves and imagination. I know that I do people an injustice, for many of them are fine and generous,

11

but it is the others who are significant. It is their thoughts one uses as a standard when one is a minister's wife.

And I wonder where Albert is in all this. Right now he is getting lines in his face — pious, respectable lines. He has a mask, and he lays it aside more and more seldom. I hate this priest, Albert, and wonder if the other one is left anywhere. The Albert who knocked on my window the first lovely night. Does he have any existence, or is it a body without soul, which at night testifies against his morality lectures? When he sinks back in the pillows afterwards, does he lie constructing lectures about purity, and freedom from the earthly? Does this doubleness go to the very bottom of his psyche? Perhaps his psyche is cloven like the root of *Orchis maculata.*

I shall dig this out. I shall see how he fasts in Lent and I shall note it down. "Behold, we go up to Jerusalem" — yes, and I shall have my notebook with me. I want to see how he washes the feet of his colleagues; how he looks upon Mary Magdalene when she breaks the alabaster cruse of ointment; how he watches in Gethsemane (perhaps he is awake some time when I am sleeping; he talks a great deal about the need of the world but in general sleeps very well and snores considerably); how he carries his cross and suffers with patience when he has a headache. It will be very interesting to find out what he really believes about the cross and the resurrection and all that. Sometimes he talks as if one ought not to take the dogmas too literally. I want to know *what* he takes literally. The marsh of ambiguity should have some kind of bottom, if not a moral at least an intellectual one.

I have armed myself. From the very beginning I have been irritated by the professional superciliousness of the ministers in the area of religion. Ask an innocent question and you are answered by a pat on the back. Once during a ministerial session I asked if they really believed that Jesus went up into heaven and was sitting somewhere up there in the blue. I sensed the irritation among the smoking brothers as they talked about being anchored in the heavenly and eternal and such stuff in order to close the ministerial ranks as soon as possible and to continue the theological merry-go-round where Latin terms and other refinements whirl around in a dance by themselves while all of reality dances in the other direction.

Yes, I have armed myself. I do not want to be taught in a spirit of humility. I am delighted to disturb the good Albert while he discusses theology with his colleagues, even though he does not do this very often. Questions of clerical advancement and administrative detail seem much more important to him. Nevertheless, on the questions of the Christian faith I shall not be silent in the congregation. I have been reading my Bible during these three years. I am not entirely ignorant of Aulen and Nygren. I think I have read more theology than Albert since we came here, but I am not any more convinced for that. I am armed and the struggle will not be too unequal. Of course, I shall never be more than a dilettante in the theological field. I lack the philological base, but I have some idea what it is all about. And, therefore, I can attack when needed. My best weapon is my pagan thought. This has not been so dulled by ministerial symbolism that it cannot penetrate a Christian heart. Reality with clear colors — come and be my friend.

When I now read this again I find that in some way I have anticipated judgment. I believe that Albert is as split as his ministerial collar. I believe that I will hate him when Lent has reached its end. Hate him as wholly as he himself is halved. I believe that I will irrevocably say farewell to my

13

calling as a minister's wife. He can get a divorce if he will, but I must save my soul.

Nevertheless, nothing should be judged without trial, neither Albert nor his religion. But there is nothing wrong with considering them as the accused and the seriously suspect. I shall accuse them of deceit — with intent to poison. Now if I can only hold myself free from phrases and prattle! I want to be as sensitive as litmus paper, as penetrating as an acid, as alert as a wren. There is a song in Sunday school that goes: "In the holy Lenten season, give me opened eyes!" If I could pray, I would pray this. No, it is not a prayer but a command to my eyelids and my pupils. A command of utter preparedness to the watchman of my soul: "Opened eyes! Opened eyes!"

2

Ash Wednesday

On Wednesday, Albert held a Lenten service in the school at Forsby. Lundberg, one of the vestrymen, was there squeezing his fat frame into a small school desk. A couple of other farmers were also there and some old women. The teacher, a woman, played the organ for the hymns. In between, she sat swallowing Albert with her eyes. I recognized that manner of hearing a sermon. The good Fröken Andersson would probably not grieve if I drowned. She would see to it that Albert was comforted.

But what am I saying? Poor Fröken Andersson probably does not understand the nature of her religious interest, and I have no reason to be jealous of her. Furthermore. it is ridiculous to be jealous.

In any event, I also listened to Albert's sermon with the greatest attentiveness. I hid it in my heart. I did, and we shall now bring forth that precious document.

The text treated the incident in which Christ sent a couple of disciples to Jerusalem to get a room where they could eat the paschal lamb. Albert used a detail in the story — it says that the disciples would meet a man with a pot of water and that they should follow him into his house to make inquiry. Albert suggested that the man must have followed this route rather often since Jesus knew that they would encounter him. He could be recognized rather easily by the pot of water he carried; in the Orient this is not men's work. It was, nevertheless, this man's daily task. And without his knowledge this task now became a part of sacred history. Thus our faithfulness in our daily vocation becomes a way for Christ into our homes and communities.

One might have expected that Albert would say a little more about how the man in the text performed a task commonly assigned to the wife. Lundberg, the vestryman, has a small thin wife who has to go to the barn for water many times a day. In the barn there is running water and a pump, for it is the men's job to water the cows. But don't assume that little Fru Lundberg can get running water in the kitchen. There is no money for that. Nor is it thinkable that the fat Lundberg would trouble himself to carry water into the house. In this parish that is woman's work. So is a lot of other burdensome toil. The women here become thin and gnarled. They wither and become angular like clothes hangers.

But all this was forgotten in the sermon. To have said anything like it would have made Albert unpopular among the men, of whom a couple are pretty influential. It is not certain that Albert had made a prior calculation and had decided ahead of time to avoid the hazardous subject. I think he does these things unconsciously. But this means that he does them with his heart. He feels heat and veers in the opposite direction. He has promised not to be an offense to anyone — and he must think of his career. To be an associate in an annex is not too bad a spot for a young priest. But next year there will be a vacancy in the pastorate for a rector.* If Albert does not apply for the position, the people will interpret it as a lack of self-confidence. If he does apply, his doctorate may gain him a nomination, but he will have to compete with the vicar, who is older but rather popular. If he fails, it will be remembered when he tries again, and it will be remembered just because he is associate in the annex.

We have never talked about this but it's sort of in the air. I notice that it determines much that Albert does and does not do. In the first place he must be careful not to become the center of controversy. To be eccentric is dangerous. The man who stays in the middle register does best — the one who says what he is expected to say, that is, who says nothing definite. This Albert knows. He knows that it might be hazardous for him to disturb the taboos; he knows this without thinking and therefore he avoids them as surely as a bat steers clear of

---

* The smallest administrative unit of the Church of Sweden is the pastorate. The modern pastorate comprises one or more parishes and is headed by a rector (*kyrkoherde*). Normally the rector is situated in the main parish of the pastorate and may be assisted by an associate (*komminister*) or a vicar (*kyrkoadjunkt*). In populous parishes there may be several assistants.

Small parishes affiliated with the pastorate are called annexes and may or may not be served by resident pastors. In *Holy Masquerade* Eriksson is rector of the pastorate and parish of Skogsby, Albert Svensson is associate of the annex Sjöbo, and Englund is the vicar of Skogsby. A rector responsible for the supervision of several pastorates in a diocese is called a "provost" (*prost*) or dean. In this translation the terms "provost" rather than "dean," and "vicar" rather than "assistant" are used.

In the event of a vacancy for a rector, subordinate clergy may make application for candidacy. The election is conducted by the parish. Vying for the office of rector is one source of tension between Albert and Englund. —Tr.

telephone wires. The wings have their special sensitivity. Repulsion is built into the motion itself. That is the impression I get when Albert preaches.

Therefore a clerical protest against female slavery in this parish never materializes. To carry water and tend the garden and milk the cows — this will remain the lot of women here even if Christian charity dictates something else. The Christianity that urges men to bear one another's burdens will find its voice on that Wednesday when there is no imminent pastoral appointment, no fear of competition from a popular free church pastor, and no vestryman present who has signed a note for the pastor.

Otherwise I must admit that Albert was right in hitting hard for fidelity in our daily work. I am thinking of his office. No poet could give greater devotion to his poems than Albert to the data that must be submitted to the district bureau every Monday. Oh, he may grumble about the endless detail of the new regulations. He can describe eloquently what must be reported when a parishioner is married and moves away at the same time. First a blank must be filled out on him showing that he has married her, then another one to the effect that she has married him, then another on him that he has moved, then another on her that she has moved, each form with birthdate and birthplace and addresses for all parties. But when Albert spreads himself out over this typically masculine red tape, something in him purrs with contentment. He loves these paragraphs and forms and this multiplicity of parish records. He is proud of his ability to control this apparatus as a boy may be proud of his mechanical know-how.

Hence, no matter what one may say about his care of souls, not even the angriest rabble-rouser could suggest that his office work lacks justification or is a matter that anyone could handle.

I must admit that he can, with the best conscience, praise faithfulness in the little — in a certificate of age or a summary for the statistical bureau. But when he said that it is in this way Christ can come in among men, I had to object. I oppose the manner of speaking, first of all. He doesn't mean at all that Jesus would come to us personally as a bishop comes for a visitation or my father-in-law comes to call. He means something about the doctrine of Christ and following Him. But if this is what he means, why not say that we become more Christian and that Christianity in general is furthered through our fidelity in our work. Why these murky ways of speaking: "Jesus comes," "He dwells among us," "Invite Jesus as your guest," etc., etc?

I asked him about this as we walked home. He answered that Jesus is present among His followers in a different sense than, for example, Socrates or Mohammed. I asked him in what way, and he took his refuge in the mystery of the resurrection. This mysterious business is always irritating. It is a place where all can hide. I suspect that it is theological fog and not much more. I said that. Albert became angry and said that I want to be impressive with my intellectualism. He was so angry that he stuttered. At that I answered that if Christ really dwells in some sort of psychic phenomenon nowadays, it certainly cannot be in this kind of theological irascibility. And I continued by reminding him about Kristin.

This Kristin lay dying in a little cottage a few miles from here. Albert and I had visited her a few weeks earlier when we happened to pass that way. The old woman had real anguish of spirit. She felt, she said, completely condemned. She thought herself to be a great sinner. "That's not so serious," said

Albert. "Mother Kristin has lived a respectable Christian life all her days." The woman protested. She was really beside herself. Albert talked about God's grace and forgiveness. But nothing helped. When we left, Albert promised to come back. He went back once. I learned from her husband a few days later that she was still filled with anxiety and that she longed for further visits from Albert. She thought she was destined for hell and had committed a sin that cannot be forgiven. It was probably that old stuff about the sin against the Holy Spirit that was haunting her. I felt sorry for the woman and reminded Albert several times to go back. But he had too much to do. He had to make some summaries for the Central Statistical Bureau. He had to send a big package of forms to the district office. He had to execute twenty-five certificates of dismissal. Kristin was left lying with her sin against the Holy Ghost. At last I could not contain myself any longer but decided to visit with the woman a bit so that she would forget about hell for that time at least. So I made my way up to the cottage. But when I came to the crossroads up in the woods I saw a stooping figure a little ahead of me. It was an old man who was pushing a cart with something oblong in it. I stopped suddenly, and then I saw who it was and what it was that he had in his pushcart. There was no use going farther, for this was Kristin's husband pushing a heavy load in front of him. This work he was doing for his wife. But he was not carrying a pot of water. The raw wood gleamed between the trees of the forest. I suppose he planned to paint the coffin himself.

I reminded Albert of this. I asked if he really meant that Christ had had any help from his office work that week. Did he really mean that he would have hindered Jesus from visiting his parish if he had postponed his statistics for a day? Now

I was so zealous that I began to use his pious jargon. "It was the 7th," said Albert, "and the report was due on the 8th. You know how hurried I was." Thus he did not answer my question. He defended himself against an implied accusation. But it did not remain implicit long. I stopped and looked him straight in the eye. "Albert," I said, "you don't believe in the Last Judgment. You believe only in the provincial office and the Central Statistical Bureau. If you neglect your statistics, you may get a rebuke from some bureaucrat in Stockholm. If the negligence is repeated, it may even go so far that the rebuke is repeated by the diocesan chapter, and that shame you cannot bear. But if you do not prepare those people for death who later appear in your obituary statistics, you will not be criticized, for this does not appear in any columns and is not noticeable in any statistic. Such matters are only recorded in heaven and will be known only on the Day of Judgment. And for that you don't give a farthing, Albert. It doesn't concern you. Hence, the only sensible conclusion is that you believe in the Central Statistical Bureau, but you do not believe in the Last Judgment. But if there is a Last Judgment, you will be accused for the murder of Kristin's soul and you cannot clear yourself, for there are witnesses to your conduct."

Albert siezed me by the arm. "Be quiet," he said. "Someone may hear you." And with that I had him as in burning pincers.

"Precisely, Albert," I said. "Your God and judge is what people say — what emerges in gossip and what is apparent to paper shufflers — and for that reason you don't give a fig about souls. For souls belong to the things that are not seen, Albert. Unseen, at least, are the souls of old women and the souls of old men. You can't recruit them for an organization or count upon them for a petition in this life. They belong to

21

another life and this does not interest you at all, Pastor Albert Svensson."

Albert told me to calm down, that I was much too tense and took everything literally, etc. I answered that it was really none of my concern, for I wasn't the pastor in this congregation, but what did concern me was if I was married to a man or to a pudding.

I saw that it hurt him. I wanted to comfort him, for he had such a pain in his glance. Tenderness welled up within me, but I hardened myself. First there must be clarity; otherwise comfort is of no avail.

That evening he wanted to make love. He seems to believe that bodies unite what the spirit severs. It happens often that he desires sex instead of admitting that he is wrong. This is painful. Furthermore, it is a whole year now since I got any pleasure out of our sexual life. I find no rest within. My whole being is tied in knots. And now during these days of the great searching, I can't do anything. I cannot love him with my body and penetrate him with my soul. We shall have to fast now, literally, both he and I.

When he understood that I wanted to be left alone, he went out. A little later I heard the clacking of his typewriter. He had gone back to the office. But I buried my face in the pillow and wept.

3

Invocavit: WHEN HE CALLS*

I HAVE NEVER BEFORE FOLLOWED ALBERT SO FAITHFULLY on the circuit as now. This time we went to Eng, which lies as far as Forsby but in another direction. Fröken Andersson was there that time also. The text dealt with the footwashing. When I heard her praise the sermon afterwards (we stopped for church coffee at the Lund's in Eng), I thought the word "footwashing" very significant. The flattery was such that it polished Albert's shoes, and Albert ate it up, of course. I sensed how greedily he sucked in all the empathy.

On the way home, we had company with this faithful listener. There were hence fewer stumbling stones for Albert along the way than last Wednesday. He did not think that he should let her go alone so late at night, and he offered to walk her

* *Invocabit* is from the introit for the first Sunday in Lent. It is taken from Psalm 91:15, "*Invocabit me, et ego exaudiam eum,*" which is translated in the RSV, "When he calls to me, I will answer him." Hartman's rendering of this introit as *Invocavit* — the perfect tense — is an error common to several Lutheran service books. —Tr.

home. She also suggested that she had some sort of problem she wanted to ask him about. I did not want to obstruct the question box. I went in and meditated on the sermon. I had barely closed the door before a name came before me with such force that I felt as if I had been pierced through the heart. It was the name of Englund.

Englund is vicar to the rector, and now when the rector is ill, Englund is rector *pro tem* in the parish. It is, of course, natural that he, who is situated in the main parish, takes care of its responsibilities, but if Albert and Englund had difficulties before, Englund's temporary promotion has not helped the situation.

The matter came to a head during a council meeting in our manse a couple of weeks ago. Normally, if the rector is absent the associate is chairman of the council of the annex. But now Englund was along and Albert had to leave the gavel to him. This did not make Albert any more passive during the meeting. He polemicized strongly against Englund in the main question, which concerned a new organ to be built in our church. Englund is baroque in his taste and wants a so-called Bach organ with its fusion of clarity and harshness. Albert wants an organ with strings and sentiment. He feels that people in general like the romantic and ought to have it. He didn't express this clearly at the meeting but he talked a great deal about folk art. This did not help. Englund emerged victorious and this bothered Albert a great deal. The two colleagues seem to have held a rather stormy after-meeting. Since that time they have not spoken to one another. They take care of their official duties by correspondence and this helps them to omit everything personal in their letters. This is called objectivity.

It struck me now how well Albert had preached on meekness

and brotherliness. If the mind of Christ would prevail, all conflicts would be solved and there would be peace on earth.

To be sure. But how can Albert say such things without thinking about Englund? How can he have the effrontery to stand and talk about the solving of conflicts while he himself communicates with Englund only ex-officio? I felt the contradiction like an ache within me. This time I couldn't satisfy myself by querying Albert theoretically. I too have a responsibility for the relations between ministerial families. I understood that I must do something. After I had thought over the matter, I telephoned to Englunds and invited them to Sunday dinner. On Friday evening I told Albert.

He looked up from the form he was filling out. He looked surprised and offended. He said that he expected to have something to say about such a decision. I told him that he would not have to cook the dinner. Then he said that it was not very suitable on Sunday because it was his turn to preach at Skogsby. But I pointed out that if he had not been serving at Skogsby, Englund would have been there and then we would have had to wait for him instead of Albert. Furthermore, he would get home in plenty of time for dinner. He said that he might have some official duties, but I had already determined that nothing of this kind had been scheduled. In any event, I said, he could keep a couple of hours free for the dinner.

He bent over his correspondence and wrote, wrote, wrote. The fact that we had our little meeting in his office permitted him the opportunity for this kind of retreat. He sat on his office chair, which both revolves and tilts, surrounded by all of the apparatus that he loves: the typewriter on its movable table; the telephone with its spiral around the cord and a patented device for numbers, attached to the desk; in addition

25

a paper punch, three kinds of rulers, paper scissors with stork bills, rubber stamp holders, ink pads, ink wells of ebonite, rubber erasers; a complex seasoning stand with paper clips, needles, hooks and eyes, and thumb tacks; and I know not what else. And then these massive church records majestically masculine and impressively arranged on the desk. This is half of Albert. There he sits swinging and tilting on his chair, smoking, writing, checking, dressed in an elegant smoking jacket. The carefully tailored coat is hung decorously on a specially complex type of clothes hanger in a little clothes closet beautifully arranged for this purpose. All of these office accouterments are a sort of continuation of his nails and his hair, limbs without feeling, detachable and impersonal, but limbs nevertheless.

Playing a part

I certainly confronted him where he was most at home. This probably contributed to my directness. I did not want to let him get started with his scissors and his stamps and his rolling furniture. (I have a feeling that his collection of evasions is related to this apparatus.) Oh, no, I thought. We'll proceed to cut all these insensitive layers of skin. We'll get in where the blood flows. And I told him that the real reason for his difficulties with the dinner should not be sought in the pulpit at Skogsby but here at home in the organ loft.

The shot went home. He moved immediately from the subject of our discussion to more essential matters. "Don't you understand," he said, "that I have to take care of my responsibilities without interference. Englund has nothing more to do with this parish than I have to do with our tenant's old Ford. And it won't be Englund who will be forced to hear the organist play his wooden preludes Sunday after Sunday. That will be my responsibility and I want no more of this much-lauded harshness." I began to understand that I was in for an extended musical-political discussion and it was not what I wanted. I consequently decided to cut still deeper and I said that if Englund became rector of the pastorate he would have a responsibility for our parish as well.

Albert began writing again. The tips of his ears were red. Was he really writing?

He got up, took a large parish record in his arms and carried it into the archives. As he did so, he said that Englund could wait to act like a rector until he had been properly elected. That dear brother ought to have some sense of shame.

We were getting near the flames. I asked Albert with what kind of behavior he had tried to counter the rectorial pretentions of Englund. I said that I found his and Englund's tactics comparable.

At this point Albert took out his cigarette lighter, a new and remarkable brand, and began smoking in earnest. He tilted and rocked his chair. He did not invite me to smoke. Ministers' wives are not permitted to smoke.

He began to talk with a new intonation, softly and courteously, with a constrained and weak voice. A volume in inverse ratio to the intensity of his fury, suddenly turned toward me. He said that he had long since ceased to expect any understanding from me in religious matters but he had thought that I would be personally loyal to him. Now it seemed that even this had been too much to expect.

He hurt me terribly. I would have liked to have given up the fight and to have fallen back on the nice watery loyalty that had almost killed me. But I had to speak the truth. I was a little angry now also and I had enough courage to bend Albert's eyes toward me. (At that moment he had them fixed on something in the ceiling.) "It looks to me," I said, "as if I

27

must choose between being loyal to your religious faith or to you. What do you propose?"

He looked merely quizzical. Then I reminded him of his sermon on the footwashing. I quoted what he had himself quoted effectively several times: "And dissension developed among the disciples who should be considered greatest." I asked him if he had not thought about a more immediate application than the fuss between the first apostles or between denominations, political parties, and African tribes. Hadn't he said that it was we who should learn meekness and assume the mind of a servant? And I continued to quote: "The kings of the Gentiles exercise lordship over them and those in authority over them are called benefactors." I pointed out that one could just as well have spoken of pastors. I continued — it seemed peculiar to take so many Scripture words in my mouth, but it was necessary since I was operating on a priest — and I developed his own intonation. "But not so with you. Rather let the greatest among you become as the youngest and the leader as one who serves."

"That is an entirely different matter," said Albert in his most pedantic tone, and then continued in irritation: "If you ask me what I mean by this, I would like to emphasize that one does not give up justice in order to follow the letter of the Gospel. One can debase oneself but not his point of view or his office."

There are, believe me, many attitudes and offices among these Christians. To provoke ordinary worldlings may have its perils. But to provoke the pious is like sticking your hand in a hornet's nest. And when there is occasion to talk about brotherly love there is usually a "point of view" or an "office" that must not be offended. It would be interesting to know where the Christianity is to be found that makes people conciliatory and peace-

28

ful. Last Wednesday Albert had said that if all men became Christians even wars would cease. Indeed! It is possible to be tolerant to the point of dishonesty. But when it is a question of protecting an old feud or even a temporary irritation, then the points of view turn red and white and one's convictions stick out like long stingers.

I did not say this to Albert. It was enough to point out to him that I had not invited an opinion to dinner and not an office either. I had invited some human beings. Then he would have to determine for himself who is the greatest, "he who lies at table or he who serves." (It was that part of the text that had given me the idea for the dinner.) I thought it would be interesting to see which of the two brothers washed the other's feet.

Albert was silent. I did not like his silence, nor the look that he gave me when he crushed his cigarette in the gleaming steel ash tray. He withdrew himself in some way behind still another layer of dignity and well-pressed clothes. I was almost sorry the day after, but then I got to thinking about the time the governor was here to confer a medal in the church. Albert took out his most elegant jargon and his smoothest conversation and oily obsequiousness plus a pound of ministerial dignity — an indescribable mixture that called forth the reddest rebel slumbering within me. Albert even had himself photographed together with the recipient of the medal and the governor. The photograph got into the provincial paper and Albert sent a copy of it to his mother. It may seem as if this occurrence had little to do with Albert's relationship to Englund. But there is a deep connection between the two intonations that I can hear whenever I like: "I and the governor." "I and the vicar." He hasn't said it that way, at least not the first; he is not stupid. But I can hear him say it. In a sense he said it by not saying it, and I shall not forget it. He does not say, "I and the vicar," either, and yet he suggests it. It forms a repulsive duet with the other loudly unsaid.

Thus I remained steadfast. And now the dinner is over. I have washed the dishes and taken care of the leftovers. And I have put the spiritual leavings in the pantry together with the other serving dishes.

There are a few hors d'oeuvres: salmon, mayonnaise, cheese. They stand beside the wine bottle as they ought. Among ministers one can now and then tolerate *adiaphora* for dinner. It has its risks; it can become known and some have lost prize posts because of it. Now, nevertheless, the hors d'oeuvres and the *adiaphora* are standing farthest in on the second shelf of the pantry. Is there something else? Is there something I listened to with a beating heart? The mood a little strained at first. Albert talked and talked but it didn't help. He gave a little speech for the guests. "There has always been the kindliest relationship among the pastors in this pastorate. Only seven or eight miles of road separate them. . . .Too bad they meet so seldom. . . .There is so much to do. . . .But my wife and I welcome our guests most heartily." I almost choked on the wine. Lies and hypocrisy; phrases and duplicity. I was surprised that the old floor planks did not bend under us and that the table did not collapse.

Mushroom soup. Talk about poor weather and few people in church. I had said boldly there would be more in attendance if people could believe that reality was being preached. From that point it would have been possible to move to almost anything, even to the footwashing. But Albert came through with a story: the one about the old lady who felt stricken and afterwards asked the minister why he had been preaching the whole time about her. Some more stories. A quotation from J. A. Eklund to the effect that you can't fool the Christian congregation. "Indeed, you can," I thought, but I said nothing. I didn't have the strength and my attempt to get the conversation in the right direction failed. It sank to the bottom like a stone. But when I carried the lukewarm tureen into the pantry, a Bible verse was in my ears, "Oh, that you were either cold or hot." I have forgotten where the verse is to be found, but I am sure that it doesn't concern itself with mushroom soup.

Veal roast with beans. Church concepts and State Church pastors and Free Church pastors and Pentecostals. Two lights among the Pentecostals now engaged in a death struggle. I stopped chewing. Now at last I swallowed and said it was unfortunate that Christian leaders could not work together. Now I was sure the conversation would take a serious turn, but no. Neither noticed anything, not anything at all. More details about Pentecostal pastors. Excellent gravy. Tender roast and wonderful beans.

Cheese cake with whipped cream and raspberries. Stories about the provost. Stories about chairmen of pastoral elections. A priest who was so fat that he could not get a promotion. Procedures at the election of pastors. My heart skipped a beat. I asked innocently how long the rector was going to remain. But no one noticed that the question burned. No, indeed! Instead they began telling anecdotes about the rector. Ericksson's talks on special occasions. His greediness; his fanatical temperance; his hasty elevation during the twenties. Ericksson here and Ericksson there. "Wouldn't you like a little more?"

"It was so good but no more now, thank you. No more." A speech to the charming hostess. "If we did not have our wives. . . .the high calling of a minister's wife. . . .this excellent meal. Our God we thank for the food. Amen."

Coffee. Cigarettes for the men. The click of Albert's cigarette lighter. Albert's and Englund's prating about church records, communal ordinances. Albert pretended to ask Englund's
advice on a serious question. "You who are familiar with
this territory." A circle of masculine freemasonry around the
two of them. Although Alma and I sat at the same table, we
were left to ourselves. Alma talked about children and heavy
work as if there were no other troubles in the world. I said,
"Yes," and "Is that so?" and "You don't say?" We sat listening
to the other two over the demitasse. They were eagerly involved in a conversation about church records and their laby-
rinthine complexity. This was the climax of my fine revolution-
ary dinner. What fraternal communion! What exquisite and
sympathetic understanding! What elegant hosts and what an
elegant cigarette lighter!

Albert shot me a glance through the tobacco smoke. It was
ironic and supercilious. And I who had thought that he was
yielding to my initiative! Albert can bow, but to bend himself
as one must to wash feet — never. I understand that now.
Instead of penance he made a detour. Instead of plunging into
the truth in all humility, he did the opposite — he floated on
top of it. What was hidden under the friendly surface was
ignored. It would remain hidden. There would be no decision
and no reconciliation. Albert sailed on as with a flat-bottomed
boat and he did so with great skill, I must confess.

But it would have been better if they had had a real battle,
Englund and he. Englund with his old church style and his
harsh organ flutes. Albert with his folksiness and his *voix
celeste*. If they had broached the question of the chairmanship
and the repartee at meetings, if they had talked openly about
the election for rector and each had said that, in his opinion,
he was the most worthy successor to Ericksson, the air would

have been cleared. But there seems to be something worse than an open struggle about who is the greatest. This subterfuge is worse. It is eerie, for one knows that the differences that have been waved away so hastily and have disappeared will come stealing back like ghosts, hide themselves in closets, and roll skulls in the attic at night. I am afraid. Afraid of white sheets and gaseous organisms. Things that cover themselves and cannot be laid hold of.

There is so much that has no definite form. Much that exists and is felt and sneaks away. Something else frightened me when Albert looked at me in that superior fashion. It was his coolness toward me. If possibly he has opened the door a crack for Englund, he has closed it for me. His sincerity toward the other was the front of his irritation with me. Perhaps something worse than irritation. As if I had gathered over myself the concentrated ill will he felt toward Englund and everything else.

This is consequently the trophy of my skillfully planned campaign. This is my harvest.

The farewell phrases sound idiotically in my ears, "What a lovely afternoon. We must do this sometime again. The distance is not farther in the other direction. So enjoyable. So delightful, little Klara. Thank you. Thank you so much. Thanks again." I pour out the coffee grounds in the garbage pail.

4

Reminiscere: Be Mindful*

TONIGHT I AM ALONE. ALBERT IS IN FORSBY AT A BIRTHDAY party, and I am home with fever and a stopped-up nose.

I am in bed and am trying with some attentiveness to read Albert's sermon for last Sunday. I wasn't able to be along on the piece of the road to Jerusalem that he wandered in Skogsby: I had to take care of the dinner and the guests. And since I have decided to follow him the whole way, I must read what I am not able to hear.

I have never liked the story about the street woman in Simon's house. It is sentimental with all that crying at the feet of Jesus. Even the words "alabaster flask" are surfeited with unctuousness from all the sermons on this subject of breaking such flasks, as if at that time it was more dramatic to break a vial than to pull a cork out of a bottle today.

---

* Reminiscere is from the introit *"Reminiscere miserationum tuarum,"* which is translated in the RSV, "Be mindful of thy mercy." It is from Psalm 25:6 and is used on the second Sunday in Lent. —Tr.

35

But there are other things in the story I don't like. Albert talks in the sermon about being much forgiven. It is easy to understand how Alm, the fat farmer in Skogsby, must have gleamed with delight all the way to his bald pate. He comes often to church and counts his money often. A faithful supporter of the priests and of the bedbugs in the servants' quarters. I seem to see all of them over there in Skogsby creeping into the big beautiful sleeping bag of confession. Alm, Niklasson with his whisky bottle, Fru Karlsson with the tongue (I always think of her tongue as black from all the poisonous things she says about everyone), Ada Grenade, who is nagging her old parents to death, and a dozen more of the same caliber. "Oh, we are nothing but sinners, sinners." And then suddenly it doesn't matter at all that one is such a sinner. God is good; the Lord forgives; grace alone. And if needed, there is always more grace for next Sunday. Yes, even now before one goes to sleep. Whoever may object to this, it is not the bedbugs at Alm's farm. Not Niklasson's drinking fraternity. And not Fru Karlsson's gossip circle. Perhaps Ada Grenade's parents could wish a more peaceful old age than the constant pain under Ada's continually forgiven sins. "It is an unfailing refuge even for the greatest of sinners. Men may misunderstand us and close their hearts. Difficulties may gather like threatening clouds, but God's door is never locked. There is always grace, and finally in the hour of death. . . ."

I can't stomach it. Although if I am just I must confess that the business of forgiveness seems to mean something to Albert. It meant something two years ago. The organist here was also treasurer of the church and embezzled a few thousand crowns. Albert had to deal with the problem, and the fact that the organist had a wife and five children did not make it any more pleasant. There was one possibility of saving the man from scandal and from losing his job. I know that Albert wanted to do this. He had figured out which men of the church he could get to subscribe the amount missing in the treasury. The organist had asked for forgiveness of both God and man, said his sectarian wife, and at that time I must say that I thought I understood something of the preaching about forgiveness without limits. Lisa — that is his wife — came to me and poured out her grief. And even if her husband had erred, it was catastrophic that the whole family had to suffer for that reason. There was greater justice in forgiveness without limits than in truth and law. Especially in view of the fact that the man must have had difficulties taking care of his large family and a wife who had a small sense of economy.

But there was another side. Albert risked involvement if he was silent. In the newspaper he had read about a priest who had been brought to justice because he had interferred in a similar case. The big black headlines had said, "Pastor Involved in Embezzlement." Some of the columnists had made the commentary that one rogue helps and forgives the other. The memory of this made Albert terrified. He was troubled about involving a fellow human being. He is always troubled by that which is painfully clear and irrevocable. But his concern for an unstained reputation as a minister decided the matter. Forgiveness was less important.

But that time Albert was much concerned. He postponed the decision as long as possible. Mail accumulated on his desk and he forgot to get a new necktie for his birthday. He would lie awake a whole hour after he had gone to bed, which I had never experienced before. When he had sent the letter of accusation, he relented and called the post office to take it back, but it was too late. I remember that his forehead was covered with sweat as he stood by the telephone. He had lost some of his dignity. His suit coat did not hang so well. And when he went out, he lit a cigarette with matches. The cigarette lighter with which he was then enamoured lay forgotten in another suit.

But the idea of forgiveness, as the theologians call it, has more suspicious connections for Albert. He can become very angry and then forget about it. He can lose his temper and tongue-lash people, but he hates to be confronted with the results. All cracks must be puttied with an even and ubiquitous forgiveness. Otherwise he gets off the track and looks as if he is involved in a very serious spiritual struggle. Therefore when I remind him about something in the past, he usually evades it and escapes to his paper work.

It is also significant that he becomes deeply disturbed if his indulgence must choose between two parties. If one of them has offended him, that is, of course, a different matter. Then he breaks off diplomatic relations, or he behaves as he did at the great atonement dinner. He directs a warm surface stream of fraternization over the whole, while cold counter-currents move down in the deeps, divide themselves, and emerge in other and unexpected connections. Or sink down in treacherous holes from which now and then grisly thoughts like demonic submarine fish swim up surrounded by lukewarm and friendly splashes. I feel strongly that what was smoothed out last Sunday lives on somewhere and that we shall see it again.

But if his own dignity is not threatened, he does his best to avoid involving himself. I remember one time when his mother was annoyed with me for asking her for her sugar ration card. She had been living with us for over a month. She turned to him, "Now Albert, you will have to determine if it is going to be this way or that. Do you think that your old mother deserves such treatment? Please tell me if I am still at home here, or if I am going to be looked at like a paying guest at a boarding house." Not only the ration cards but a whole lot of more sour matters got into that discussion.

Albert sat under his mother's verbal lashing and looked from one to the other with the greatest unhappiness. After a while, when it got quiet and he had to say something, the doorbell rang. He was polite and went to open it himself. He did not come back. The ringing of the doorbell had come as a *deus ex machina.* When I got out into the kitchen, I saw that the number on the board was not "one," which belongs to the vestibule, but "four," which designates the room where we sat. Albert had rung the bell himself. There is a contact under the rug. The room has been used sometimes as a dining room and Albert was sitting where he could reach the bell. He has an amazing ability to find contacts of that kind when it begins to get warm.

Tonight he is a long time coming back. Since he is such a perfectionist, it is strange that he leaves me alone for such a long time, especially when I am sick. There have been many late nights recently. He has been occupied with his parish duties. I wonder if this is a pretext. Perhaps he feels that there is a purgatorial fire burning at home.

Has this purgatory anything to do with love? When I lie here, furious because he is not at home, I am not indifferent. A moment ago I thought I heard his step on the porch. I waited for the next step and said to myself, I shall certainly tell him what time it is. I waited to hear the soft grip on the door handle, the scraping of his feet on the mat, courteous and punctual even in nice weather, the clicking sound of the clothes hanger when it is taken down and is hung up again, the clearing of his throat when he straightens his coat. But the continuation did not come. He fills up the whole house with his absence. I wonder what I shall tell him when he comes, how I shall catch his evasions like butterflies in a net, how I shall meet his arguments, how I shall nail him down and impale him.

If he stayed away and never came back, I would be an arrow without a target. This is my situation. I shall always seek his heart. Sharp and without mercy. Is this love?

There is something in his evasions that I cannot explain by the fact that he is the son of a tradesman. He worked at his father's store and he learned that the customer is always right. For that reason as a minister he knows what goes and what does not go in our enlightened time. And if it were merely a matter of identifying and separating out from his soul these holy business methods, the job would soon be done. But I have realized that he could not take a position even if he were removed from the theological market place and could make his judgment of the whole from some distant planet. If he could evaluate religious currents for a periodical a thousand light years away, even there he would say about the Oxford movement, "It is good but it has not understood the church and the tradition." And he would say about the high church tendency, "It is all right but it doesn't have enough room for the personal and the individual." And about the neo-orthodox, "They do not concern themselves with the scientific world-view and modern man's intellectual difficulties." And about the criticism of Christianity by me and innumerable other modern people, "They are dealing with problems that theology solved twenty years ago."

It is this that is the worst of all. That his cruising mentality and his intellectual conscience have been welded into sheer confusion. We have had fiery partisans in the parish: pastors who sacrificed their career for the sign of the cross and other peculiarities, or who wore themselves into shreds for the ecumenical ideal. These points of view and perspectives are as strange to me as a lecture by an intellectual ant or a seraph in human disguise. But they are my type. They give me a clear answer. They seem satisfied with unpopularity and it gives them new edges. But Albert weighs diverse opinions against one another like nuts on a scale and says "Too much," "Too little." His skepticism and his faith are both a fog where it is easy to lose your way, for he is knowledgeable, if one can call knowledge that which lacks all fixity. But he will become rector on the strength of it, believe me.

To me this is poison. My whole being reacts against it. But I shall not be satisfied with the reaction. I intend war. And this brings me back to Albert's alabaster sermon. "This is the way it is when one loves," he says, "then one can forgive everything. This is infinite forgiveness." If he means anything by this, he cannot believe that I love him. Perhaps this is why he looked so coldly at me on Sunday. He thought that I was interested in smashing him, and his counterattack was the flanking tactic where he is a real master. He countered with "infinite forgiveness." That is to say, smoothing everything over; in that way the whole business was taken care of.

Oh, I know what he would answer in reply to this. He would say that Christian forgiveness is much deeper. Such forgiveness demands confession and repentance. This is what he demanded of his colleague before the dinner. But a little later when the diplomatic situation was a different one, fellowship was restored in the sign of general fuzziness. I am afraid that this is always true. When Albert's sermon is about to be practiced, as at our dinner, the diplomatic situation becomes fuzzy.

But if I love Albert, my love does not satisfy itself with a shallow confession or an indulgence woven of sighs and pleas. The Pharisee Simon was not so stupid when he thought that Christ should know who the woman was who touched Him. That's the way it is between Albert and myself. I am incapable of smoothing things over. I know every minute who he is. My love walks into his being with the torch of a rebel. It demanus revolution or it is unfaithful to itself. Like the Oxford people, it wants a transformation though in a different manner. It cannot shut its eyes and forget. It knows clearly who it is who touches it. Albert would say that it is blasphemous to make such a comparison. Perhaps so, but perhaps the truth is always blasphemous.

But I feel as if my love has broken its shell and has begun to live an independent life. Or is there a better word than love? Whatever it is, it rises up out of my being. It is certainly rooted in my body, and it burns with cold fire, with transparent clarity, and with merciless passion. I break my alabaster flask and there is no odor of roses or salvia. The flask contains no fragrant balm. A spirit lives in the flask, a penetrating and immutable spirit that fills up the house with clarity.

I have a fever; otherwise I could not write such solemn words about myself. Now that Albert has come in, I notice it. The proportions shrink when he is around. He forces me to permit him to deal in trappings. He busies himself with something down in the vestibule. Soon he will come up the stairs. Yes, now he tiptoes up one step at a time, avoiding the fifth one, which creaks. The fool thinks I am sleeping.

I did not sleep. The door was open. He had to look in when he went by. At present he is sleeping in the next room. He said it got late. "I noticed that," I said. I wondered what *that* was which was so late. He answered evasively: "everything," "the whole business," "the meeting." And when I tried to clarify the meaning, he became annoyed and asked if he should account for all the food served at the party and all the stones on the way. I looked at him (and my eyes are not very cloudy tonight; they are in fact larger than usual because of my fever), and I told him that I was furious about all the generalities in the small and in the great in which he indulged. I told him that I had to analyze every sentence to convince myself that it wasn't totally empty and only generalities. I said that I was afraid that he himself was empty, a large "that" in clerical dress. And that all his talk of forgiveness and what else he had said in his sermon, these things were only pretext to let him have his alabaster flask empty and without fragrance all the days of his life and unto the end of time.

Albert was silent. But it was not the same silence that sets in when I have him in the corner. There was something in his eyes that I had not found there before. "Perhaps you are right," he said, and the "perhaps" was not a portal to the indefinite. It had an element of conviction in it. Then he went into his own room, and I have not yet heard his bed creak. What is he doing? Is he sitting up and thinking about something? I can't believe that my action already has shaken his confirmed indecisiveness. Is it possible that what I have done has shattered some glass in his solid variety store even though it has not turned over any counters?

5

Oculi: Eyes*

YESTERDAY WAS THE DAY OF THE ANNUNCIATION AND TO-
day is the third Sunday in Lent, the one called *Oculi.*
I shall take it as my talisman. "Opened eyes, opened
eyes." But it's just as well to begin at the beginning. Annunciation Day is a strange bird in shimmering colors settling
down in the midst of gray Lent. If I were a Christian, I
would love that day. Seemingly Albert has nothing against it,
but that is probably because he makes it something else than
Annunciation. He preached about motherhood but did not say
a word about the problem that every thinking person listens for
with both ears. Does he really mean that it happened as the
day's gospel indicates? Was Christ really born of a virgin?
Just think if there were angels who came and made things clear
instead of talking like Albert about something else. When he
came home I attacked, of course. I asked him what he meant

* Oculi, from the introit for the third Sunday, is derived from
Psalm 25:15: "*Oculi mei semper ad Dominum,*" translated in
the RSV, "My eyes are ever toward the Lord."   —Tr.

when he recited the Apostles' Creed. He said that naturally he believed in the incarnation. God has indeed revealed Himself in the man Christ, he said. It is the whole life of Christ that is the miracle and that miracle is not made any greater because one tries as formerly to explain how it happened. Furthermore, the explanation is only a literary form for the truth of the incarnation. For that reason one can use the archaic words without lying. One really means the same as the old biblical authors.

I said that the Confession did not talk about the life of Christ so generally. It talked about a foetus in the womb of a woman, and Albert answered, "That's right, that's right. The miracle was already present in Mary's womb." Archbishop Söderblom had expressed it in that way on an occasion. The whole question is not very germane today, he continued. Theology has disposed of it a long time ago.

And he thinks that people know all about this? And that I shall be satisfied with this explanation?

I asked him why he never told the old ladies what he meant when he said "conceived of the Holy Ghost." They at least believe that he considers it in the old way. I told him it wasn't honest of him to let them believe that. But Albert was not without answer. He took out his lighter and said, while lighting his festal cigar, that, on the contrary, it would be dishonest to indulge in the sort of explanations that I wanted and they could not understand, and thus turn their attention away from the spiritual message of the day to a physiological story without the slightest religious significance. The result would be, not that they went home and thought about Christ, but that they went home and thought about two entirely different things, the virgin birth and the orthodoxy of the pastor.

So I got mine. If you can ever get Albert to break the seal

on his secret documents, it becomes clear that he has thought
through more things than you give him credit for. I had
to hunt around a while before I found the real source of my
difficulty. It was just this: he limited the miracle to the spiritual.
What had happened or had not happened physiologically is
not at all insignificant for everyday people. It was quite mean-
ingful that Albert gladly talked about miracles as if they existed
far beyond all the realities of ordinary people. This is without risk. It doesn't antagonize anyone. It doesn't concern anyone. And it's really this way with everything that is preached.
You ask: Does it really exist? Do people become conciliatory
through Christianity? Does it make any difference in business
or politics? Does it have any consequences in the psyche of
the hypochondriac?

And then I asked, "Would you be different if you were not
a Christian?"

Albert said that this was not relevant but his face got red
and he spilled ashes on the floor.

But then he counterattacked. He said that I myself believed
in the right and the true as if they were eternal verities. In this
way I had crossed over into the world of miracles, that is, to
that which is beyond time and space. But this faith did not,
he said, mean that I believed in divine healing. In fact I limited
my belief in miracles much more than he.

I reminded him that I did not belong to the teachers in
Israel. I press my lips together during the Confession. I do
not preach sermons on the Annunciation; not even on *motherhood*. I. . .

". . .thank God that I am not like other men," Albert continued. "Like church women or dissenters or like this minister."

I was silent. I did not know what to answer. He was right,
of course, that in some sense I sit in judgment of him. But

I do it to get out of a desperate situation. It is an act of defense. Furthermore, I make no pretention of being anything. I have no Christian symbols on my chest. I do not even pretend to be an honest person even though I should like to be.

But after a while, and then the coffee was ready — the drinking of coffee seems to me in retrospect a ridiculously idyllic frame for this deeply serious conversation — after a while I asked Albert what it was that prevented him from believing in the virgin birth. Wasn't it quite simply that the dogma is not considered decent among cultured people? The obstacle for him could not be the scientific world-view since he had already disposed of this through his faith in answered prayer — if he now truly believed in this.

I did not wait for his answer. Suddenly it flashed upon me, and I told him that the reason why many ministers doubt in what Gabriel said to Mary and declare it nonessential is a massive, masculine self-sufficiency. They cannot digest the fact that God has restored Eve, since during thousands of years men have blamed her for all transgressions. And anyway it was a costly restoration. But suppose it were true. Suppose it were true that one could become pregnant through a miracle. Suppose it had happened to me.

"Don't blaspheme," said Albert.

"You have no right to talk about blasphemy since you don't believe in it," I said. "You theologians never want to hear about reality. You claim that it does not mean anything or that you cannot believe in it or that it is blasphemous to air it. But suppose, Albert, that the miracle had taken place here and now in time and space. Suppose it had been I who had become impregnated through a miracle."

My voice failed me. It was as if a knife had stabbed me

when I said it, although I did not give myself time to think why.

"What do you think they should have said at home," I continued, "if I had been living like her with my mother and father? What would my betrothed have said when he discovered the state of affairs? Not to mention Fru Karlsson with the tongue and all the leering boys at the street corners. To talk about being with child through a miracle — even rather nice people would have shaken their heads and said that it was a fantasy, perhaps a fantasy brought on by lunacy or wild despair, but in any event a fantasy. The world does not believe in miracles. I know that well who am myself a worldling.

"But I go to the minister. Here comes the woman who carries the Son of God in her womb. She rings the doorbell and asks if Pastor Svensson is at home. And you, Albert, receive her in your office. I am allowed to sit in the hard chair and you sit opposite me in your adjustable chair. If I were a woman student you would offer me a cigarette, but you notice that I am only a backwoods girl from Forsby and that I am already beginning to be heavy-footed. You consider that the statistics on illegitimate births are rather high for this year. You prepare yourself to deal severely with the father of the child, who is not showing himself responsible.

"But I look at you with confidence and with joy for I feel that you will really understand this, you who are a pastor. I tell you that I have had a visitation by an angel and you think to yourself, Aha! she is a Pentecostal or a peasant. As you sit with your back against your well-ordered filing cabinet, you find a place for me. You put me in folder five: *Ecstatics*. But you don't say anything; you pretend to understand for you don't want to disturb my childish faith with nonessentials.

"And so I tell you the story, that which is beyond all understanding. But you look at me with psychoanalysis in your eyes. You query a little here and there, and by and by you try to worm out of me what are the true facts about my condition. I begin to be frightened. Just think if not even a pastor can understand. But then I remember that I myself couldn't understand anything when Gabriel said that I was to bear a child through a miracle. And so I try to tell you that it has pleased God to send His Son into the world through my insignificant being. I can't quite understand this but I assume that you who are a pastor. . . .With the world as it is, I say, it will probably take a miracle if God is going to become one of us. But you say that if God wills, He can send His Son into the world through a spiritual miracle. The idea behind the two things is really the same. And why do we need miracles when we have theology?

"The last part of this you don't tell me because you don't think I would understand, but you give me a nice little speech about motherhood. You say that it is a great responsibility to be a mother. A heavy responsibility, especially in our day. You say that it is important to be worthy of this holy calling. But I get no answers to my question and I find no place of refuge for my secret. I look at your rationalized office, everything gleaming steel and lacquer and varnish and efficient cleverness, and I say to myself, there can't be any angels in this world of card files and punches and scissors and rulers. How can there be any miracles in the land where the ministers wear shiny black office coats? So my own faith deserts me. It is probably true what the pastor says and I stand up to go."

I actually got up. I curtsied a little for him and walked a few steps toward the door. It wasn't theater and it wasn't insanity. I thought in actuality that I was the Virgin Mary, an incredibly poor and concrete present-day Mary on her way to a social welfare agency. But when I got to the door I felt that the child leaped within me and I thought, "And so at last I am experiencing what it is to be pregnant." And I was in heaven and hell at the same time. But then the fiction burst and the tear in it went down into the flat reality. I stood leaning against the door lintel and wept so that my whole body shook. And Albert sat pale at the coffee table with cold coffee in his cup. He looked at me terrified and his forehead was sweaty. At last he murmured, "You must understand that I can't help it; it is impossible for me to believe." But then everything came to an end for me and I shrieked at him, "But then say it and say it so everybody hears it!"

And I ran away from him up to my bedroom and threw myself on the bed. Why was I in such turmoil? What does the Virgin Mary mean to me?

I began to understand that the worst thing for a skeptic is not faith but self-evidence. It is terrible to doubt when there is no real faith to doubt in but merely beautiful words. Oh, to live in a time with clear colors, when the ministers believed in angels and devils and atheists were burned at the stake just as if they had been martyrs of the faith.

Today we are back in Lent — the high churchly say that the Day of Annunication breaks the fast and lights a Christmas candle in the gloom — but for me this day and yesterday have in a peculiar way melted together into a single experience.

This morning Albert preached on the Gethsemane text. The sermon for the high mass became in that way a sermon on the passion. I have never heard him so far outside of what he said. He did not pretend to know what it is to be in Gethsemane. The sermon, all of it, was only phrases — a bit of carpentry made to order. But just this made me ask myself if there is not some sort of development under way in Albert. He has to preach as usual but meanwhile he is seeking clarity on his own — no, perhaps this is impossible. He will probably remain true to the old. But I cannot completely escape the thought that perhaps. . . . If he were just a trifle troubled over his chameleonism, as he was yesterday. Although it was probably because I wept; the tears of women are the worst thing he knows.

The morning worship was, nevertheless, very significant for me. While Albert preached I sat pondering over what he ought to have said if he had had the old faith. I was helped by our altar painting, which is a good piece of work. It shows Gethsemane with bare branches, as bare as the trees outside of the church, but without buds. It is unthinkable that they should have buds; they are frozen into some sort of *rigor mortis*. And there are some large stones, naked and objective as a modern office. In the background some sleeping men; they sleep heavily and healthily like Albert. Cold moonlight, chalk-white over the cliff, and a man fallen on the ground. He looks like a discarded rag.

His fingers are bent as if the hands were already nailed to the cross. They look like spiders ready to flee away in fear over the sand. It is God who lies there, cast aside by mankind. God has crept into mankind's anxiety. And because He is God, He has been able to penetrate more deeply into us than anyone else and to shut the door upon Himself. God cries to God and groans. An author who prays to himself for grace for a character he permits to be destroyed could do the same if he were God. But it is not a work of art God creates in Gethsemane. What He does, He does because He is so human. He cannot look upon our lunacy from the outside and say: "Poor people." He must be the rag with blood on it.

I feel a wrench of pain. There He lies who was my child yesterday, two thousand years ago. I have changed His diapers. I have patched His clothes. Like all boys He wore them out over night. I have been proud over His marks in school and anxious about His wild adventures, and now that He is grown my concern has grown with Him. I cannot follow Him any longer. I can only watch with Him while the men sleep over yonder. But I cannot — and this is hard to understand — I cannot follow Him into the midst of His trouble, for I am not God. I am only a peasant girl from Forsby. But, dear God in heaven, don't let it last too long, for then neither He nor I can endure.

At this point, Albert said, "Amen," and I awakened. Fru Karlsson with the tongue sat and looked at my makeup from the right rear while Albert thanked the God who comforts, teaches, exhorts, and warns us. I was once more the pastor's secularized wife.

Indeed, I am more and more convinced of my worldliness. Albert said yesterday that I believe in something absolute. He had not reckoned with any religious faith in me. I have never said that I was an atheist. I have never said the opposite either. I want to get some clarity about myself. But I think it very difficult to believe in a mild providence who looks down upon our earthly hell and smiles graciously in his beard; when I remember Gethsemane it is hard to believe that. The rag on the rock, He who calls God His Father, is for me a protest and a contradiction of a nicy nice faith in God the Father. I read during the war about human beings in Hamburg who, during a bombing, melted down with the asphalt in the streets. Afterwards you could see a little child's hand stick up out of the congealed mass. I wonder if it is not the horror of this sight that makes it impossible for me not to look at the Christ hands in our altar painting. This is the kind of thing the Good Father in heaven ought to look down on. Perhaps a bit sorrowful, perhaps lifting His finger like an inept school teacher in the seventh grade: "Now let's all be nice." No, that I do not have strength to believe.

But what about my absolutism with respect to the right. Perhaps it is a variant of this bland faith. You put God a little farther away and change Him into a neuter; in that way you don't have to reckon with His heart.

And nothing of this can be proved. Perhaps we can talk about a tendency in man to transcend his limits and to create ideals. Then God turns out to be the same as man's striving, a direction toward which man's spirit stretches like a cactus in a window. Perhaps so. One thing is sure, there are clean colors for man. There is a black and a white. There is a straight and a crooked. By this simple law I want to live. This I know and can prove. But I am not sure that I want God smuggled into it somewhere.

I am also convinced that my experiences in no wise mean that I am becoming a Christian. Since I was a child I have often wanted to be someone else. And I have sometimes made the game into reality. Why does one have to be an actor to identify oneself with something else? To move out of oneself for a time? Or to be compelled to do it, when one is gripped by something?

I know why the Christian values grip me. It is because I am by nature a worldly person. I need a faith to doubt in, and when I cannot get one from Albert, I have to make one for myself out of the stuff that I have learned to know now during the last three years. And if I am going to follow Albert to Jerusalem, I have to live myself into what he should have lived himself into, otherwise I cannot judge his lack of consistency. I must think about Christ in order to understand the pitiable in Albert. I must do this to understand if he is beginning to take his Master seriously.

And I notice that the light of my unfaith casts a shadow, a sharp and movable shadow when I recognize what faith believes in. Most of those who think that they doubt do not have a legitimate unfaith. They have only a sweet little child doubt. You have to be a pastor's wife to reach the height of doubt, and if you are not married to a priest but to a compromise, you have to complement him. And this is what I am doing.

6

Day of Penance

I HAVE BEEN ILL, VERY ILL. I WAS APPARENTLY CARELESS with the cold I had last week and I developed a fever and a sore throat that made me think about the camel and the needle's eye every time I tried to eat. It is remarkable how Albert's interest for me blooms when I am ill and I must make some demands upon his concern. There is almost something of guilty conscience in his fussy coddling of the patient. Or is this something that I imagine — but there is also something else. His way with a pillow case reminds me of my childhood when my mother fluffed up the pillow for me. He wants to treat me like a little child and I object to this. I don't want to be cared for and dependent. There is also something unspeakably irritating in the assurance with which he gives me my medicine, offers me my invalid diet, brings me novels to read, puts out the light with the exhortation that I should sleep, and awakens me with honey water and the thermometer on a tray. This assurance he has also in the kitchen when he broils cutlets or stirs batter. He is an old scoutmaster and likes to show off. There was a time when we joked about this and he called me Proud Wolf because I wanted to take care of myself.

But it is no joking matter when one discovers such peculiarities to be the essence of the man one has **married**. Something essential and alien. When he meets an old schoolmate, he works through all the common acquaintances, "how it is going for them": if they are married, if they have children, if they are happy, if they have any prospects for promotion, if any one of them has an uncle who has been in a sanitorium, or married a vocalist, or become a Pentecostal. In all of these situations, Albert asks how it's going. He doesn't care about their points of view unless these are a help or a hindrance to a career. A clergyman who makes the sign of a cross or is a Social Democrat unfailingly provokes an interested, "No, you don't say?" Not because this may lead to a discussion of theological or political questions but because this may affect "how it goes" for the person in question. I consider this despicable. I can almost hear him talk about himself as some sort of third person. "Svensson? Oh, he married a doctor's daughter from Big River. He was only an assistant then but she seems to have had some money. Now he is an associate in Sjöbo — there's to be a pastoral election there soon. We'll have to see how it goes. He is not badly thought of in the parish, but a great deal depends on what they say about his wife."

It's probably stupid of me but I think he has all of that with him when he comes with his thermometer and his honey water. "How's it going? Do you feel better? Your cough doesn't sound good. Are you taking your cough medicine? There's nothing better. You will notice how it loosens your cough." Factual, detailed, curious, friendly. With a thermometer.

I am probably mean, who cannot appreciate his concern. I want to be honest and to repent. Unfortunately, I cannot change myself and really like his pampering. It was a day of penance a couple of weeks ago. I had to go home to congratulate my father who was sixty-five. I shall probably have to have a day of penance for myself and not for Albert. For at the same time I intensely dislike Albert's care, I am terribly ashamed about feeling as I do. And I remember very well how angry I became last week when I thought that he neglected me.

I tell myself, "Remember all the flowers Albert has placed in your room. Think of his concern that you will have enough money for your household budget, that you are dressed properly, that you shall find a comfortable chair to sit in during the coffee after dinner, that you will get three pairs of nylons the day they go on sale at Olsson & Son, that you will have the most delectable pastry when we go to the city. Erase from your mind all the times that he has wounded you with his silence or his intolerable finger pointing, for afterwards he has often asked for forgiveness with a bottle of perfume or a collection of poems. In any event, he has not done it in the bedroom by seducing you in a very deferential manner or by not doing so; he has retired when you are weary or have your period."

It is impossible to repent. I have tried many times to be nice to him. I try it almost all the time but it is not honest. It is only an official recognition of his goodness. There is always an undertone of irony even when I say, "You are such a dear," or "Thanks for being so nice."

There is, nevertheless, a part of me that loves the touchingly helpless in all his well-packaged concerns. I remember a time when it was so cold in the church that he was afraid that the Sunday school children would get chilled. He took them into

59

the parsonage and arranged twenty-two chairs for them in the parlor, beautifully ordered in semi-circles. During the lesson a little boy from Persgard wet his pants on our nice parlor rug and began to wail in terror over his misfortune. Albert stopped the lesson and let the children sing a long hymn. In the interval he took the boy with him into his office and put a towel in his pants. Then he put him on his knee, and took his handkerchief and blew the child's nose, which was certainly needed. The boy forgot his sorrow and became interested in Albert's clerical collar and Albert permitted it and changed his collar later.

I saw it all, even though Albert thought that he and the boy were alone. It hurts me to see paternal anger in his movements. I see this tendency in much that he does. Sometimes it seems less paternal than maternal. He has very soft hands.

It surprises me that he does not take this manner with him when he visits the old people. It is only youth and childishness that can awaken his protective instinct. That's why it blooms around me in situations when I am ill or when I hand myself over to him in love so that he can say, "My little wife," and comfort me the way one does a child when it is about to sleep.

But I have not given him a child and I cannot myself be a child for him. I wonder if the fact that we do not get any children is related to our use of contraceptives before we were married. He wanted to protect me, of course, and I didn't long for any children at that time. Not then. Now I think about it with a feeling of guilt. I wanted to be a pagan in the sexual. Even so, I was afraid of what people would say if it became known. A pretty pathetic kind of paganism, I can see now. We certainly need pagan days of penance also when we confess sins against our own flesh.

The doctor says that perhaps I could become pregnant if we adopted a child but I don't want that and I don't know why. I feel an aversion to accepting help from the outside. I don't want to be fruit-bearing through an ingrafting. Albert says that I am a Pelagian because I don't want to live by grace either from God or from men. I want to be my own.

It is perhaps this that makes me reject all the pampering. There is a bouquet of anemones beside me — Albert brought them home yesterday. A little girl had told him where they could be found. These childishly humble blooms represent everything that I cannot become. Their line is neat and proud, childish and seraphic; they look like the line of the sun in the sky at this time of year and they are idyllic in their blueness. "The little anemones." I see that it is beautiful but I can't bear it. My meekness has another line, which does not bend itself toward the earth. I despise the sweet.

In spite of this I was glad when Albert came home with them. There was a touch of spring in them and when he handed them to me he was touchingly proud over his find. But I stiffened and my "Thanks, dear" was a clanging symbol, metallic and impersonal. There is something in me that is chilled by this sort of gesture. As soon as I see it, I consider it gauche.

Albert noticed this and was wounded. I heard it in the sound of his typewriter when he returned to his office and began to work. It sounded energetic, determined, upbraiding. I thought to myself, I'll let him take me like a sweet little flower. And in the evening I pretended to be someone else. I chirped like a Madame Butterfly and laid aside all of my intellectual panoply. I wanted to do penance by breaking my fast and

61

throwing away the scourge. I didn't want to be a Jerusalem pilgrim any longer. I shut myself off from the large perspectives and tried to limit my vision to the bedroom.

I lay in the light of the lamp with the green shade and there sat my husband who had come up to tuck me in and say goodnight. The blind was drawn before the hostile eye of the window and everything was quiet. Only the water pump throbbed now and then and an occasional car ground up the hill outside the house. I pulled his hand down under the covers and caressed it. I felt that my body could perhaps soften, obediently permit the warm waves to cover my skin, obediently abandon itself. Stop thinking, don't pull up the blind. Perhaps I can lift myself toward him like a handful of flowers that he thinks is so wonderful; lift myself with body and soul, at least in pretense, in gratitude for the roses by the wayside.

But he must have noticed the hypocrisy, for he took his hand away and said, "Now you have to sleep so that your fever will go down tomorrow." Once again concern, thoughtfulness, and tucking in. "Good night, sleep tight."

In despair I lay in the darkness and let shame creep up my fingers, my arms, my throat. I had wanted to pay because I cannot receive anything for nothing. But what do you call paying for this with your body? Peculiarly enough there are situations where you are caught between two ways of doing wrong. If I do not repent, I am proud and self-righteous. And if I repent, I am trying to pay for what cannot be paid for and with something that one cannot pay with. I must confess that in this connection I understand what the Christians mean with the talk about grace and atonement. But if anything is false, it would be to close a day of penance like this by becoming a penitent before God, as they say in the chapel. The miserable little part of me that understands that kind of talk would have all the remainder of my personality as an auditorium if it crawled to the cross and prayed for grace. And it would be a very skeptical auditorium. The only penance that I can make is to confess how it is: I cannot repent.

I could not have written this last night. The shame that crept around in my body was not caused by the sudden insight that I was false, but also by the humiliation of being rejected. I knew that I had no right to give way to such a feeling. I had personally closed my door in Albert's face for several weeks. I can't ask that he shall interpret the message of a caress, especially when it is a lie and deception. Furthermore, I ought to be thankful for his thoughtfulness. The temperature is raised by aroused passions. Nevertheless, I feel as rejected as if he had preferred someone else. Oh, the idiotic wisdom of the body, which constantly fills us with unmotivated feelings!

I sometimes wonder if our faith in God is not a confusion of feelings generated by our glands. Man stands alone under the stars and longs to be made part of someone's collection of valuables. But no one cares about him and he feels insulted. He says there is no God. And there is as much of a sneer in his voice as there are bitter drops of rejection in his blood. He goes to all who will listen and says, "There is no God." But no one believes him, for his anger testifies that there is something or someone who has irritated him. And this way faith has come about through the wisdom of the body, which is willing to give itself but receives no answer under the stars.

But there is something here that does not fit. And since I have set as my goal this time to impose penance upon myself and not upon Albert, I must acknowledge it and note it. Grace — the grace about which Albert preaches now and then but in his application changes to an eternal smoothing over — this grace cannot be an invention of our glands, for the God who tucks His great starry blanket about us and spreads the heavens over us in a sibling bed with quislings and queens — this God our instincts have never lacked. He is too unreasonable or anti-reasonable to be a construction of our intellect. I confess this: there is a temptation in this — a temptation to believe because it is contrary to all reason.

But I cannot believe. I do not have the strength. I stand on my own shore and see faith like a continent on the other side. It is not my country. I live in time and space and common sense and in a land where you get nothing gratis.

All would be well if I could pay. But all I can do is to write a debit sheet

Debit: Albert is kind toward me and I despise it.

Credit: Thankfulness in word and act that I do not mean and Albert does not want.

I have the anemones on the table beside me. When the spring sun flashes in the window, there is a little aura of purple around them and in the high church they say that purple is the color of penance. Perhaps my coolness toward the flowers is caused by this. Perhaps I could enjoy Albert's kindness with my whole being if God were not between us. I cannot straighten out our relationship with one another without landing in God.

But whose God? Albert does not believe in Him, at least, I feel, not consistently. And I am an atheist, I think. But I find purple everywhere. In my home town the police once apprehended a thief by sprinkling aniline on some bank notes they had hoped he would steal. That evening he was arrested outside a cinema. He refused to accompany the police. They showed him a pocket mirror; the man had wiped the sweat from his forehead with his stained hands.

It is thus with the fast of my ungodliness. Here I am and I

am innocent. I analyze and lay bare. I am confident in my common sense morality and integrity. I find myself unaffected by hypocrisy, at least in the essential. But then something flashes before me and I see the color of purple cast upon my thoughts by the antependia and the chalice coverings. It is well that no priest sees it, for then he would say, "You were with Him. . . ."

But I can't believe it.

7

Laetare: REJOICE*

THE GOSPEL FOR THIS SUNDAY IN LENT: FIVE THOUSAND hungry people are fed when there is no food to buy. Report for this year: "Of the young people in this city, 75% suffer from acute tuberculosis. The cause is primarily lack of food." See the picture on page three in the same paper: a child with a swollen abdomen and limbs like the branches of the trees in Gethsemane, a big head, bottomless eyes, and hands like. . . .No!

---

* Laetare is from *"Laetare Jerusalem,"* in Isaiah 66:10. The phrase reads in its entirety, "Rejoice with Jerusalem, and be glad for her" (RSV). This is the introit for the fourth Sunday in Lent, which is also called Mid-Lent, Refreshment Sunday, Mothering Sunday, *Brotsonntag* (bread Sunday) in German, and *Dominica de panibus* in Latin. The reference to bread is drawn from the day's gospel — the feeding of the five thousand. In England the "simnel" or "mothering cake" was distributed on that day. It was a simple cake, intended to break the monotony of the monastic fast. It survives in the Scandinavian countries as *semla* (L. *simila*) or *fastlagsbulle* (Lenten bun).   —Tr.

Albert did not preach over that text. He talked about a text that dealt with the denial of Peter. Peter is a very popular apostle. Even Albert likes him very much. Albert talked about the temptations of the gray morning. The first temptation: to deny Christ for the opportunity to get into the house of the high priest and to superintend the Christian interests in the world. Second temptation: to deny Christ because most people are His enemies. The beloved Peter was surrounded by a hostile circle of people in front of the fire. Third temptation: to deny Christ to evade responsibility for what one has done. The last one who made Peter fall was a relative to the one whose ear Peter had chopped off.

Albert talked almost as if he knew what it was to deny Christ. He was in it himself; it almost made me gasp. "Who has not at some time compromised his Christianity to please the world . . . all of us know how easy it is to be pulled along by the masses, to speak and to act against our conscience when we are drawn and beguiled by a bad example: 'Everybody is doing it' or 'That's the way it is nowadays.' All of us know the persuasiveness of the voices in our inner man when the evil passions hold council. . . ." It sounded pretty genuine. And it was also genuine when he said, "How easy is it not to fall. How persuasive is not the world." We all felt sorry for Peter who was so compelled to deny. We indulged our weakness and wept a little out of sympathy for ourselves. In Albert's sermon.

I didn't think much about it then. I was a bit affected by the realistic tone of the sermon. I found the whole thing humane and understanding. I thought the mixture a bit strange: the bread gospel, the denial sermon, and the litany.

But afterwards I gave it more thought. We were invited to Alm's for church coffee, for Albert was preaching in Skogsby that Sunday. There were almost as many there as in church; among the guests were the church wardens and their wives, the merchant Gren and his wealthy wife — he himself is bankrupt — Bogren, the choirmaster, with his wavy hair, farmer Nicklasson of the bottle, and Fru Karlsson with the tongue. And noticeably present: the coffee table. A damask cloth on the enormous oak surface, mirroring multicolored sparks from a crystal chandelier. A coffee service in sterling. Rusks, a coffee cake, saffron bread. Cookies, Fru Alm's most noted creations: gingerbread, sprits, butter pastries, almond cookies, Finnish sticks, sugar cookies, meringues, fudge bars. Jelly rolls, sugar cake, and ginger cake. With his first cup of coffee, Albert said that there was clearly no rationing in this area. This while there still remained the cakes for the second and third cups of coffee. A whipped cream cake, high and white, like a snow-crowned mesa, weighed down by two centimeters of foam. Further, a mocha cake from the best bakery in the city.

I sat before a cookie mountain piled on my plate on top of riverboats and pagodas as if Fuji had spewed out all this fragrant white lava that had congealed into flat, twisted, scalloped, finger-like, kidney-like, heart-like, brain-like convolutions. Fru Karlsson with the tongue came and sat beside me and the rich Fru Gren. Praised the jelly roll and Alma Englund. "She is so simple and sweet." Fru Alm, who has some sort of noble blood, agreed from an adjacent table and pointed out that Alma came from a "good family." Despite this she is so common. I sat there with my worldly makeup symbolizing all types of levity, boxed in among the true brothers and sisters of Christian denial. The conversation continued about ministers. The Reverend Mr. Borg who had been in foreign service and had seen a number of concentration camps. The Tongue pointed

69

out that it was difficult to see that he had ever visited any famine districts.

With that I was far away. I remembered some slides Borg had shown one night when he held a lecture here. Long gray arms that looked like pistons rather than limbs. Eyes staring with hunger. An open garbage pail in which some half-wild children were grubbing. I saw the great and glorious cream cake among gnawed bones and dead rats with hairless tails.

But Fru Karlsson awakened me by pointing out that I hadn't done much with my cookies or with my coffee. "It was the same way with Fru Englund one time at a baptism some three years ago," she said. That was when Alma was carrying her youngest.

At the same time Fru Alm saw my plate and in her coaxing finally arrived at the great modesty of her party. She stressed that she had nothing more to serve than one could find in the country, which "of course" wasn't very much for those who were used to other things.

I know that I am not accepted as one of them. I am only a city dweller on vacation, three years' vacation. But this was too much for me. I was in despair that I could not get out of the trap. Whatever I said would be misinterpreted as conceit or patronizing praise or pregnancy. But I was suddenly struck by the thought that I ought to state things as they were. "I was just thinking about those who cannot share in this," I said. "Oh, they're eating in the kitchen," said the stupid Elsa Gren. And Alm, who certainly knows what is said about the menu in his kitchen, was not sitting far enough away to miss what was said. His bald head turned crimson. But I could not prevail upon myself to break the point of my involuntary attack.

I continued by saying that the train of thought I had

developed here at the church coffee had already been actualized in church during the gospel. I said that it did not seem so senseless that there is a text about Peter's denial on the day of the feeding of the five thousand. What I now saw before my eyes was the fourth denial. This happened on every Sunday and in every parish, but today the circumstances were worse. I couldn't be as smooth and understanding as Albert. I said that I thought about many who had no kitchen to eat in. I thought about them *also*. I wondered if it were right for us to eat cookies in such masses when there were children who had to look for their breakfast in the garbage cans. I told what I had heard about suffering and such things from people who came from Hannover to our church coffees and Lenten sermons. I wasn't the only one who couldn't swallow all the cakes, I said.

There was absolute silence. Fru Alm's face was like stone. Fru Karlsson with the tongue looked around her with burning eyes.

I know what Albert thought, "There goes the pastorate of Skogsby." But he was the first one who rallied. He rose up to his full height and looked over the congregation in his pastoral manner. And then while he rolled up his napkin and held it like a diploma in both hands, he said, "My wife's words could easily be misunderstood. You know, all of you, that we bake cookies at our house also, even if we cannot achieve the same class as our hostess today."

Class, class. He knows very well that I am not at all awkward in practical matters. But in this situation it was more important to flatter Fru Alm than to be just toward me. He had the pleasure to see her face soften by the suggestion of a smile.

After a polite bow in the direction of the hostess, Albert continued, "I agree with my wife that when we are treated in this extraordinary manner, we ought to think about those who suffer need and privation, and it is appropriate that we thank the Giver of every perfect gift for His grace toward us and our country, that we have been able to escape war and famine."

That's what you call a free translation. They sat there now with their hands already folded and their faces worshipful and devout. Just think that one should thank God for one's own escape and not be disturbed over the sufferings of others. Sit behind mounds of goodies and think, "Thank you, dear Lord, that I have not had to die of starvation like Germans and Frenchmen and Poles." This kind of thanksgiving belongs to the most selfish elements I have discovered in Christian piety, and that's saying a whole lot. It hugs itself before the spread table and finds everything in its proper place. "A delightful universe. Here I am with my food. Thanks, dear God." And this was the sort of gratitude Albert wanted to impose on me. It was treason.

But while I sat and thought about this, Albert talked on. When I awakened again, I had a great surprise: he suggested that we take up a collection for the Red Cross. Through some clever turns he suggested that this had been my intention with the meditation about the cake plate. He got them all to believe that I had sat there ruminating on a talk for a collection, motivated by "my known interest for the Red Cross," as he said. It was, he concluded, in the grip of a double anguish before the suffering of the world and the necessity to beg for a collection that I could not swallow a single cookie.

What a masterpiece! The strained atmosphere was dissolved by an act, a beautiful act at low cost. The collection was taken in an old hat. In it you could put as little as you wanted without being noticed. You could put in a farthing or a crown. In the old days, the indulgence was certainly costlier.

I saw new life in the faces and in the hands. There was a festal clinking in the large purses. There was joking about the hat. It was wished that it would be more difficult to count the money than the hairs usually found in the hat — since the owner was bald. Evidently the displeasure that I had caused was about to be overcome. Perhaps Albert had saved the pastorate for us.

But while I sat thinking thus, I was gripped by a peculiar anxiety. I didn't feel that I could sell my opposition for a pittance to the Red Cross. And while the money was being counted I felt with increasing clarity that I could not permit Albert to deny the truth in my place. Yes, the word "deny" came, in fact, before me, even though it did not have anything to do with Jesus or anything like that but was only honest anger.

The collection was thirty crowns and a few pence. I am not going to mix in the silver coins from the story of Judas here. It was not, as I have said, a question of Christ, and I had no discipleship to sell. But in spite of this the number came like something spectral into the situation. I could not give my consent to this. I could not, I could not.

When Albert had thanked for the offering, the Tongue said that now I could start eating my cookies. I said that I didn't think thirty crowns would suffice for all the hungry. Without thinking about it I had talked in the language of the miracle of the loaves, and Albert took the opportunity to add a few words about how the little can be blessed so that it avails for many. I said that if we were going to talk about Biblical parallels to this situation, we ought instead to talk about the parable of the rich man who lived every day in joy and

73

splendor while Lazarus lay outside his gate. But I shouldn't have said that, for now fire was kindled in Fru Alm. She said that the words "every day" were the most shameless she had heard in a long time. For in her house everyone toiled every day for pork and potatoes and went dressed in working clothes. And Alm added that if one were going to scrape together the leftovers from the meals that some people eat every day in the week, there would be a pretty large church coffee.

I thought that Alm's hired men would not get much of those leftovers in any event. And Elsa Gren supported the whole with a new commentary out of the wellspring of her thoughtlessness: "Yes, indeed, thriftiness is a virtue."

Albert tried to save what could be saved and said that the matter of superfluity and poverty was a very difficult ethical problem, and many learned men had struggled over it. It is not only a question of food but of money, furniture, and clothes as well. Even our fine homes. There is a shortage of housing in the world and many have no roofs over their heads. In addition to every other kind of privation. Under these circumstances one could ask what it is right to own and to keep. Could the words of Jesus to the rich young ruler to sell everything and to give to the poor really be applied to our time? For us, he said, the Lutheran concept of vocation is very determinative. We believe that it can be a calling to be rich and have everything and yet to hold it as a steward. Let us consider what would happen to the national economy if we followed the advice to the rich young ruler.

I thought it rather curious that the word of Jesus has never been applicable to anyone except Catholics and fanatics. It was apparently intended only for the young man — he must have had a monstrous love for the earthly, since according to traditional interpretations of the Scriptures his possessions imperiled his eternal welfare, whereas people like the Alms did not need to feel any concern.

But Albert chattered on. It was clear that one did not help the displaced by moving into the woodshed, even though sensitive people found it difficult to live, for example, in a large manse during a time when many. . . .

So now I was a *sensitive* person. He indicated that I was noble to the point of scrupulousness and wept over the fact that our rooms were not filled with Germans and Poles.

Whatever I said, Albert made it into a moral-philosophical problem or a dogmatic question or an indication of nervousness. Anyway, I began to feel ill before my cakes. I felt that the crumbs were beginning to move like worms. I rose up and said that we had to go home. And the others followed my example. "Thanks" and "Nothing at all" and "So very pleasant" and much else followed in beautiful confusion. I hurried. I had to get out for air.

Albert sat quiet in the car. He appeared tired and sullen. When he got home he said he didn't want any dinner. I said I could understand why. Sometime, I said, we had to have a fast. He stopped in the midst of an about-face. "Fast?" He looked at me ironically. "Fast? Aren't you thinking of getting yourself a rosary also?"

I became furious and pointed out — for I don't know which time — that it wasn't I who stood for the Christian values and traditions in the house. But it nauseates me, I said, that it never occurs to a pious person to let the proud, pious words touch reality. You fast for forty days and you have a mid-Lenten party at Alm's. In the Lenten hymn we ask: "Who goes to watch with our Lord?" — and then there is a line which follows: "to taste the cup of anguish." Thereupon one lays down a few coppers in a collection basket and one goes

75

to church coffee and eats a mocha cake from the bakery. The Monk. This is the church, the body of Christ, about which it is said that "if one limb suffers, all the other limbs suffer also." When we talk about suffering or hunger or poverty in the church it sounds so serious, but Alm never has to be afraid of sacrificing any money to the suffering and the hungry and the poor for it is always a question about spiritual testings and the soul's hunger and the poverty of the spirit. Everything is just as serious as the hazarding of "goods and honor and life and all" in a hymn. "But the pastorate of Skogsby, you, Albert, are unwilling to hazard," I said.

Everything came out of me in a flood. Albert stood and smoked during the outburst. Looked out of the window. And was silent. Absolutely silent.

Suddenly he turned around. "Perhaps I could hazard it some day," he said, "if I had a wife who really intended to be my wife and did not leave me in the lurch."

And he went his way. I understood. The accusation was turned back upon me. What I had said about the church applies to me. For me, my wedding ring is as empty a symbol as the host in the communion — there are no realities behind them that mean anything. This is probably how Albert's thought-process would have looked if he had continued it to the end. But I cannot admit for a moment that he is right. Have I not been faithful? Have I not permitted myself to be buried in this poisonous life for his sake? Is not my hatred of the lies that surround us an expression of my duty as his wife?

That we do not have any children means that our life together has something of a symbolical character. It cannot be permitted to be mere flesh, as the Christians say. But this is something I can't help. It can be his fault as well as mine.

There is much that should not be mere flesh. Are not these

notations a substitute for the acts that would actualize my doubt? To analyze Albert, to oppose him when he wraps himself in his holy diplomacy, to go to church with a bit of cosmetics, and to refuse to eat the cakes at church coffee: these things are not effects of a true opposition to God but mere reflexes of my negative love for Albert. My doubts never become pregnant; they bear only abstract nouns. Or is it just this, that on my ride through my nightmarish world I cannot find a true refuge where my doubt can give birth?

If I were a free person, I would have gone to the masquerade last night. Old friends in Stockholm had in jest sent me an invitation. When Albert had gone out for a while, I know not where, I took the invitation out and wondered how I would have dressed. I have always liked dressing up and it was especially tempting to think how I would have gone to this secular party, this masquerade at the family Söderström. In the midst of Lent.

During the evening I felt the desire to have a little masquerade for myself. Why not? I went up into the attic and took out some old clothes and drapes. I stood before the large mirror in the bedroom and tried. I was many, I was no one. A drape over one shoulder, a short skirt, a curtain rod: I was Athena, the virginal huntress sure in my spear thrust, sure as the truth when I threw my spear — or Agag, the friend and enemy of the proud King Saul, who encountered the sword of the barbarous Samuel with the words, "Surely the bitterness of death is past" — or Barabbas, the rebel chief whom the people liked more than Christ, a man I would have liked to know — or with a softer draping of my veil and with a flower in my hand instead of the curtain rod, I was the Virgin Mary. I thought of how she looks, up in our church garret, sculptured in wood by Albertus Pictor. I hung up a mirror on the wall behind me so that I could see myself from the rear. The veil did not fall naturally and I could not make my eyes so large and deep. The nose and the mouth are identifiable without a mask. But there was something wrong with my left arm. I held it in many different ways. I draped myself with it. I held it against my bosom. Then I discovered it was only the child that was lacking, the child on the arm of the Virgin.

When I took off the veil and the skirt and put on my own clothes I felt that they were not my own. I wasn't myself; I was someone I represented. In the same moment I looked at the mirror from another angle and saw the second mirror in this mirror and in the second mirror I appeared also, as I was in the mirror within this mirror and in another one within that and in another one within that and another one and another one in an eternal series. I drowned in myself, but in spite of this the I that I drowned in was only a frame for something I could not get a hold of, something that fled, something like Albert, something like Albert's faith. It was like a sermon on hunger that is not a hunger after food but a pure sermonic hunger, a hunger for a hunger for a hunger, *ad infinitum*. It was Lent with church coffee. It was "spirituality." I don't mean that I thought of it that way. I experienced the whole thing as a bottomless mire. I don't know how long I stood that way and then fell down in the deep that was myself till I managed to get a hold of a bottle of perfume and throw it at the mirror so that there was a hole surrounded by long cracks where I had been, a grave for the masquerade.

So the day ended that had begun with the denial of Peter in the church at Skogsby. Is there someone who denies and someone who is denied? And who is denied by a masquerade?

8

Judica: VINDICATE[*]

FOR A WEEK NOW I HAVE BEEN LOST IN MYSELF AND CANNOT find my way out. I want my reality to be univocal. I want my I, my ego, to be all one piece like a good linoleum, the same on the surface as on the underside. Therefore, I have declared war against Albert's ambivalence, this faith that warts to be skepticism and modernity, this fast that gourmandizes, this morality that understands and forgives. I want a single center for all circles, I want one and the same thing in what I do and say and think and dream, one single thing in the inner and outer, the physical and spiritual.

But Albert has confused me by questioning my integrity as his wife. I have defended myself by saying that it is impossible to be one with him who is many and still be one. To be married to a conglomerate is to commit polygamy. And

---

[*] *Judica* is from Psalm 43:1. *"Judica me"* ("Vindicate me") is the introit for the Sunday before Palm Sunday. The full text is, "Vindicate me, O God, and defend my cause against an ungodly people; from deceitful and unjust men deliver me!" (RSV). —Tr.

when I married it was on the assumption that I was to live monogamously. My struggle concerns this: to avoid being married to several men. In this struggle my body and soul are a single indignation. I am in focus.

This was my first reaction. I thought that I had disposed of what Albert said and added it to the minutes. But it has come up again. The reason for this is what I experienced that night before the mirror. The reason is my secret masquerade.

I have always thought of it as a game, this business of dressing up and being someone else. But I always thought it was the same person who wore the different masks. But now it seems to me that all I wanted to represent by dressing up is a series of mirror reflections. The one within the other and within me. And this I, which mirrors itself, does not stand outside the mirror any longer. The I is drawn into the eternal reflections. The masked is itself a mask. And if this is true, I am as many as Albert and it is pharisaic of me to pretend to be anything definite when what I am is merely an attitude.

This is not a "result," something that I know. It is a yearning within me, a large hole in my mirror self. When I write it down it is to see if it seems plausible. I do it in the hope that it will appear to be a novel or like a sermon. For example, about the demoniac — the one whose name was Legion, "for we are many."

But I don't know. I think of Albert's office where a paper with a few marks on it can be so terribly important. This comic apparatus that gives Albert such an illusion of weight and reality. Just think if my clear image of reality and its science and criticism of dogma and love of truth, just think if all this is only a shell around *my* contradictions and evasions. What I call "realities" is *my* office, and my struggle for an either/or in Albert's and my life is only a long pair of paper shears or an impressive stamp that I use to make myself impressive.

Perhaps what I want to be has some significance. If I wear a mask, perhaps it is because I *want* to be like that. This comforted me for a couple of days. I felt firmness under foot. For what I want is not only a series of decisions here and there. It is not like peas falling out of a bag and rattling around on the floor. It is a ruler that runs straight through everything I do. And if so, then there is a coherence which is I.

In other words, I would not have become nauseated before my cake plate at the Alms if I had not wanted to carry the mask of social sympathy. Apparently I affect my will even physically. And now when I find my silver fox less soft and pleasant than before, it is because old Fru Aronsson came here with her mission bank yesterday just as I put the fur on to go out. For Fru Aronsson offers to the mission in the same way as a man who spends half his salary in the saloon. Something shines in the old lady when she comes. She goes into this enormous act of self-negation — for it is not a question of small sums — as if she were going to a feast. And when one sees such a spirit of sacrifice, one feels ashamed about a silver fox. Especially if Albert manages to look a little ironically at it and, in his inner self, watches for the results of the mid-Lent Sunday in the realities of my every day. For this is what he did.

I would like to be like Fru Aronsson and a half a dozen other ladies of the similar type. Not so believing and churchly as they, but just as filled with integrity, honesty, and solidarity with mankind.

But I am not sure of this. Isn't it possible to think of a consistent hypocrisy? If I want to be a saint today and a slut tomorrow, I am a hypocrite. But if I want to be a saint all the time, then I have chosen my mask and I am that. But there is something here, I think, that is out of kilter. If you say that you are a harmony of all you have within you and all you want to be, that's not right either. For there is such a diversity of melodies within me. I don't know how to go out or to come in.

For that reason, I have not investigated Albert so much lately as I did before. I am looking inward too much. There is a possibility that consistency is pharisaic, not inconsistency. For soon I think that all is possible. His ambivalence, his fear to take a position, can be a kind of honesty. Perhaps it is all the other masks, the other "truths" that hinder him from choosing one. He would consider it hypocrisy, for the others are he also. Instead, he is seeking for some sort of collective rule for them all.

In reality, "person" means "mask." I learned that in theology; when one talks about three persons in God, he is talking about three masks that God puts on when He shows Himself to us. I have looked in a Latin lexicon for the word *persona* and have determined that it can have the meaning that the theologians give it. Friday, I asked Albert directly if it is not hypocrisy when God shows us one *persona* in creation, where there are praying mantises and tuberculosis bacilli, and another *persona* in the life of Christ, where the sick are cured of their bacilli.

Albert has been angry with me since the Alm episode. He hasn't said much more than the minimal but has gone about brooding. Now he answered in an open and friendly manner as if he were happy about the resumption of diplomatic relations. He said he didn't know. "Sometimes it looks rather strange," he said. Was he no longer able to stuff all his problems into this theological system?

I said that if God is a hypocrite, we should not be surprised if religious hypocrisy is so general. "Why just religious hypocrisy?" he said. And added that if existence itself is contradictory, people will naturally be ambivalent.

These are new notes. Is Albert really agonizing about the inconsistency in himself and in existence? Just think if Albert should arrive at something entire and I should become uncertain and splintered. Although I don't think that I, like God and Albert, can carry around three masks at the same time. If I go to pieces, I go to pieces.

Not to know who you are — perhaps this is hell for those who have been too curious and have looked too deeply into the mirrors of their being. Perhaps this is the unhappiness that follows upon the sin against the Holy Ghost that Kristin thought she had committed. To meet eternity, as the ministers say, and not have a name for yourself, this is an anguish that no clergyman can help. There will be no name on my gravestone, I who am about to die. I do not exist — where is the absolution that will take that nightmare away? Perhaps Albert himself experiences it. Perhaps that is why he didn't want to help Kristin. He couldn't. His comfort cannot fill the great emptiness in the absence of one's self, in the absence of the ego fiction, or whatever you might call it. And can he even comfort himself? What do I really know about him?

I feel myself more uncertain than ever after the morning service yesterday. He talked about Christ and Barabbas before Pilate and the people. Missing was the usual aversion for all but Christ. Albert asked who could have behaved otherwise. Of course I consider Pilate impossible. He is everything I despise in Albert. Whenever I want to, I can see him in Albert's elegant jacket with the youth emblem on the lapel. But if you don't know what the truth is, how can you act otherwise? Not only Christ was at stake; it was crucial to make the best of a situation and to avoid a riot. The lives of many were involved. If right and truth are not objective but only masks that you wear because you happen to like them, how can you blame the diplomat? If one day truth is dissolved in me — which I sometimes fear — it would be dishonest to deny it. Then it is more honest to deal with each situation in terms of its practical consequences, and deplore that it could possibly lead to the crucifixion of Christ. Even though I did not need to wash my hands and place the blame on someone else. It is possible to assume responsibility even though you don't believe in any eternal laws and thrones of judgment to be answerable to. But if Albert blames something on Englund, and I criticize him for it, he can answer, "I know what I am doing. I assume responsibility for blaming someone else." If there is no truth, the story with the mirrors is there again: I assume responsibility for the fact that I assume no responsibility and where is then the one who takes responsibility? Only a reflection? Perhaps I could be a Pilate, but then I would become insane.

I played Barabbas on the Sunday in mid-Lent, so I know that I could be he. Albert asked who could abstain from such public favor and defer to an unknown fanatic. I have never been interested in popularity. But I have yearned to be a chieftain and proudly receive the acknowledgement of the people for an honorable fight. To receive my freedom in order to resume the fight: I would have done that. And I understand all that is implied by "letting Barabbas go." I rejoiced once when Albert took me without permission of the church. In spite of everything, I probably felt the same thrill of freedom and adventure when I invited Englunds for dinner and when I rebelled at Alm's. Yes, I can be Barabbas, spit on the laws,

84

love a woman, and raise a rebel army. I could march by the Nazarene, the unarmed, who just talked and talked, and in greeting brandish a bold sword of action.

But all this was only a play of fancy in contrast with what I felt when Albert came to the woman, the wife of Pilate. She who sent a message to her husband in the midst of the solemn manly deliberations, "Don't concern yourself with this righteous man, for this night I have suffered much in my dreams for His sake." I felt the sword within me. The Virgin Mary felt the sword. And I felt as if I had dreamed the dream. I felt as if I had met His mother and said to her, "What have you done with Him? You had a son and it was a miracle that you got Him. You had a hard time at first but you carried Him with pride. And you fought your way through. And now look what they are doing to Him. Couldn't you have taken those ideas away from Him in ample time? Couldn't you have given Him a sweet girl and taught Him how to build a home? For these are not things that He could have learned in the shop of Joseph. Or were you so anxious to keep Him for your own sake that you showed Him other goals, what the theologians call 'the higher goals'? He was going to be something great and you could sit at His side and hear that everything was your achievement. Look now what you have done."

There were other visions in the dream. Visions like my mirror fantasy, and every new reflection was a new investigation, a new torture, and a new instant. Were they really visions? They were panes, narrow rooms filled with a kind of heavy and suffocating gas. An endless succession of terror.

When I awakened, I sent for Pilate. Since this was a dream within a dream, I only awakened to a new dream and there he was to whom I was married. I tried to get him to take a position. I hoped that he would break my mirrors to pieces and free me from what I had seen when I dreamed. He would give me a clear and single act to love or hate. He would be able to declare a person guilty or innocent and thus to free him. But he said that most deeply seen truth is relative and that in principle the man was innocent, that he would be punished by death, and that he himself did not want any responsibility for the issue. Shiny surfaces within each other. And Albert stood in the pulpit and said that many of us would probably have acted like the diplomat in the dream, who was my husband.

Then I took off that mask and saw if I could be Christ also. I tried the crown of thorns and looked in the mirror to see how it fitted. But it belonged to someone else. It did not belong to me. It seemed stolen there where it sat like a crown of myrtle on my waved hair. I threw it away from me, afraid that someone would see that I had stolen it and would report me to the police.

I have often been someone else, but I have never been Christ. There is no traditional reverence in this, as far as I know. In this Lenten project I don't want to be stopped by that kind of thing. It isn't out of any fear of Christianity, for I need Christianity to doubt. It is something else. Oh, I find Him within the frame of my metamorphoses. He is my son and He exists in the records in my husband's office. But at the same time He stands outside all of this. He is transcendent and I do not understand why. Perhaps it is because I see Him now and then in the pupil of the mother. How does the Virgin look at her son?

To have a son is to carry something of your own on your arm and yet to live constantly in a birth process: he has to be separated from me and that hurts, but it would be worse if he never became someone else, a man, a chieftain over his own world. Perhaps it is the Mary in me who does not want Him returned to herself. Perhaps I could get outside of myself if I had a son. If I had a focus for my thoughts outside of myself, perhaps my own self would be open and simple. It would not be a crooked room where the rays bite each other in the tail, but a well of light with straight beams, beams with a beginning and an end. Otherwise I don't know why precisely Christ should become so essential for me. At least as an orientation point for my criticism. And so alien, so inaccessible to my art of masking. Perhaps the key to my mirror problem is here. I saw Him involved in my own and I saw Him outside of everything, outside the Pilate-I, the Barabbas-I, the Mary-I and the whole masquerade.

This was so strange that it did not leave me all that day. In the evening when I was alone again, it made me nervous. I began to think of the old madonna in the tower. If I was ungodly enough last Sunday to play masquerade, perhaps I could go out to the madonna with a candle. The one is not crazier than the other. And I cannot leave any track untried in this investigation. So I got hold of a candle and I went out. There is no electric light in the church tower. When I went through the gate between our manse and the churchyard I felt like Dr. Jekyll, who tomorrow would be Mr. Hyde. It was I who closed the gate, someone else would open it again. Someone else closed the gate and after a while I, as a sensible modern person, would open it again.

I put the church key in the lock and opened the door. I lit a candle in the portal — the scratch of the match echoed between the stone walls. Then I walked up the creaky old stairs and beside me wavered my gigantic shadow. I opened another door and I was in the tower chamber. The carpenter had left some shavings and scraps of wood on the floor. Nails rattled over the planks when I struck them with my foot. The whole floor creaked as I walked over to the large wooden madonna in the corner. There were thick layers of dust on her; I put the candle to one side and wiped her face with a rag. Someone had cut away her chin and on one cheek there was a large spot of tar.

I picked up the candle again and lifted it toward her face. Had Albertus Pictor been able to solve the riddle? Empty eyes stared out into the darkness. The smile on her lips was for distant objects. There was an asymmetrical character to the muscles of her face. She was not conscious of the child in her lap. She did not wonder if the child had taken enough milk from her breast; she would not put her finger in the boy's mouth to feel if the first tooth was more clearly defined and sharper than yesterday. She had seen something else. . . .

A shudder went through me; the candle flame fluttered. Suddenly with terrible clarity I saw that she was insane. There was nothing that gathered together her idiotic smile. It had been lost somewhere within her, somewhere in space around her.

I stood absolutely still and stared into her face. Then I tore myself away and half ran over the creaking floor, down the steps, out through the door where the candle went out in the draft and the gigantic shadow died beside me.

But all night I saw her smile.

9

Palm Sunday

S NOW HAS FALLEN AND IT IS QUIET AS AT A FUNERAL; THE
white takes away all sound. The light cuts into the eyes in
a special way and when you touch something out of doors,
it hurts your fingers. I felt it when I broke willow twigs for
the altar this morning.

I went up to the tower again and looked at Mary. In reality
it is stupid that I have to seek for her there. When I read
what I wrote last week it sounds romantic: to go up into a
church tower with a fluttering candle in my hand. But, in fact,
this is what I must do to learn what the old church art has to
say about Mary's problem. There are many of these old wooden
madonnas in the bell towers in this country, for this is the
artistic interest of the clergy at present. Now I went up to
see if the cold morning light substantiated my feeling that
Mary was insane.

But I got no such impression. When the light fell on her
from the north window, she suggested words in the old psalm:

"The look of simplicity and the faith of innocence." And when I tried to get hold of what had looked like madness, it struck me that she resembled someone I knew. I searched in my memory but recalled it first when I was down in the church fulfilling my traditional duty as the minister's wife. (It wouldn't be so bad if my only duty were placing flowers on the altar.) When I turned around I saw the face in front of me — not Mary's but one that I had seen there by the altar once during a communion. It was a young farmer's wife, one of the quiet in the land, and she had a radiance close to that of religious ecstasy. This is perhaps also a kind of madness. I don't know what I am going to call what I myself have experienced today. In any event — if Mary was this way often, what happened to her child is not strange.

It is difficult to write down everything in the order it happened, but I shall try even though I am full of turmoil within.

At breakfast I told Albert that I had seen a figure of Mary where the saint looked as if she did not have all her faculties. I wondered whether he had heard any interpretation of this phenomenon; but no, he had not. I suggested that it could be a question of ecstasy. Albert became thoughtful and said that possibly it could have some connection with the fact that Mary often symbolizes the church, "the mother who bears and nourishes each Christian" — the quotation is probably from Luther.

Yes, I said, that is possible. For the church has certainly turned away from this world. She does not see the world. Therefore she cannot take care of children either, for mothers have to have their eyes everywhere. Mary has neglected all of us, and Christ she neglected most of all, I said.

Albert said that he thought my opposition was directed toward something entirely different. I used to talk about the church's compromise with the world and question her consistency in the heavenly and the spiritual.

But I would not permit myself to be fooled. I reminded him that the church as a religious concept is one thing; the church that engages in parish politics and carries on intrigues in pastoral elections is something else again. In fact, this is a sort of madness. The church suffers of schizophrenia. She is split and the part that prays and preaches does not know the part that neglects Kristin for the work in the pastoral office and quarrels about organs with Englund and eats cakes in Lent. Or it could be called bigamy. The church has one love at the altar and another at the telephone. I don't remember everything verbatim. Albert parried by asking if the sexton hadn't come in to pick up the notices. Apparently he did not like the subject.

But I did not yield. I said that modern people ask for singleness. Whereupon Albert asked if I myself was univocal. How should I answer that? I was quiet for a time and looked in my mirrors. But then I pulled myself together and said that I wasn't any church. I said that modern man is not single but just for that reason he asks of the church that it shall give him something to believe in or doubt in. That the church shall save him from his Chinese puzzle: box within box within box; that the church shall stand outside the ambiguity, and not be itself a mass of layers and an everlasting something inside something else.

It was time to go. Albert rose, thanked God for the food, said that he had to go to the sacristy to see if Englund had come. Englund was to help with the communion today. Albert considers it tiresome to be alone even though there are not so many communicants here on Palm Sunday as there are in Skogsby on Maundy Thursday. On Thursday he will help at

Skogsby, so that Englund will not have to distribute both the bread and the cup.

Englund's communion meditation dealt with the text about Christ giving His life for a ransom. He said that all of us needed to be ransomed from the slavery of sin. I have heard that before and it doesn't move me. I don't feel like a slave and the priests don't either, for if they did, they would not accept both their sins and a great deal else with such tranquility. If they believe what they say they would never have another glad day, for, according to orthodox faith, most people are chained in the great slave train that every day comes nearer hell. But they don't believe it. No, they don't. Although sometimes I wonder if Englund does not, for Alma has said that he has a long intercessory list of people for whom he prays every day, as if this can help. In any event, he continued by saying that the host was like a coin in appearance and in its effect like the atonement of Christ. For the bread was Christ Himself. It is the ransom in which the life of Christ was gathered together like sunlight in a magnifying glass.

I shuddered and thought that if I had really believed that the two times I went to communion during my hypocrisy as a minister's wife, I would not have dared come near the altar.

And then Englund stood and read the gospel about how Christ like an ordinary laborer rides into Jerusalem on an ass. He jeered at all splendor and glory, while wearing vestments gleaming with gold and gilt, an ornate hymnal cover from the 1880's. When the sermon hymn was sung and Albert appeared in the pulpit, I began to think that what really means something to me in the present accounting is hardly what he says but what he doesn't say, for there is the essential Christianity. It is this that I want to see in the face. In the beginning it was Albert that I wanted to follow on this Lenten pilgrimage, for

I thought it was from him I should beg my freedom. But I cannot see myself against the background of Albert's compromises. I have to have a proper contrast. The question no longer concerns me and Albert, but me and the Christian faith. On the basis of what I experienced later I could say that it concerned me and. . . no, I can't say it.

Albert began by defending those who cried Hosanna on Palm Sunday. He said that Christ understood how weak they were and knew what they would do on Good Friday. Even so, Christ let them carry on. It is never forbidden to hail Him, said Albert. It is the same way with communion, where the church even today sings Hosanna. The people with weaknesses and frailties have the right to receive, for there is forgiveness of sins in the gifts of the communion. "Come to me, all you. . . ."

But he named an exception: Judas. The communion cannot be used as a hiding place for a hostile attack on Christ. We cannot go there if in a few hours we intend to betray Him. There is no absolution for sins we intend to commit. It is, of course, rather common to condemn Judas. But there was something peculiar in Albert's way of repeating these points of view. There was a tremor in what he said. There was the ring of seriousness. Just think if my atheistic action should lead to Albert's salvation.

The actual communion mass followed. Englund has a little ritualism in his veins and he did not share with Albert what is central in a mass. He read and sang it alone. He took the bread and the wine to the center of the altar and blessed it with his hands and not merely with his words. I thought when he took the bread that if he believed what he said about it he would hardly dare to touch it. He would feel as if he had got hold of a burning coal and he would stammer the words he read and his hands would tremble when they lifted

93

the chalice. They would tremble so that the wine would be spilled on the altar cloth.

The two priests knelt. They were going to say the Lord's Prayer. Between them stood the paten and the chalice. Daylight from the outside gave the silver the color of milk and etched a chalk-white square on the altar painting. I sat upright and observed. I was filled with this peculiar drama in which gestures and words have been preserved since the time when they were real. I felt that something incomparable and personal like a line in Picasso or a phrase from the music of Schubert could be found in this breaking of the bread. Something that no other could have done, no other, then. . . .

I had hardly finished thinking this when I saw it. I saw it in the white square on the white stone in the Gethsemane painting. It was directly above the chalice. A face with large eyes — they were like wells. The face was not pretty: it was too narrow, it shone golden-brown in the dark mass of hair, and the beard made it seem longer than it was. But it radiated an incredible power, not like that of other men but like. . . . It was a completely alien power, quiet in intensity and fusing the mildness of women with a sternness that was like the sea or an open hearth in a steel mill.

At first I was ready to explode. I got tears in my eyes and my heart pounded. But then I thought, this is not true. This man is dead. He cannot be found in time and space any longer.

I got up and stepped out of the pew. I went slowly down the aisle. No, the face did not blink. No human being can hold his eyes open so long. His eyes looked at me but they did not move when I moved. Not a wrinkle in the forehead or around the mouth changed. The nostrils were still as if they were made of wax. It was not a man, it was a picture. I knew that. My eyes deceived me. I projected an ikon on the wall.

It was probably a memory from some museum, which moved out of me and shone like a stereopticon image on the white square there in the distance.

When I woke up I was standing before the altar and the ministers were standing there too. They had ended their silent prayer that Albert wants to conduct after Our Father. He looked surprised and probably wondered if I thought that it was time for the communicants to come forward.

I turned around and went back to my pew. I saw everything that happened. I saw that Albert was trying to catch my eye before he turned around to sing the *Agnus Dei*. I saw those who went up to the altar. I saw that Fröken Andersson had a spot of wine on her white blouse when she returned and that Lundberg, the church warden, wiped his mustache with his large tobacco-stained handkerchief. During this whole time I also saw the ikon, although I now saw it in a different way. I thought: so I am really mad. I have a split personality, or I have a tumor on the brain. I see what does not exist.

But I see that I see it. Someone stands beside me and says to my eyes: you see a lie and a falsehood. That someone is I. And both the ikon and I are outside the mirrors when our eyes meet. *Cogito, ergo sum* — no, *dubito, ergo sum*. I was outside the drama of the church. I doubted in Christ. I was also outside the masquerade. I had no mask. I was only will and thought. I could have believed my senses — that possibility existed, but I chose the other. I myself chose it. It was just at the intersection, at the crossroads between faith and doubt, that I became outside all masquerades, a naked doubt before the ikon. If this is insanity, then the insanity is closer to the truth than the drama in the church and the spectacle outside the church. To be beside oneself is to be outside the mirror play and to be oneself.

I don't know if I want to be operated on for this clarity if it sits in a tumor. Even though it hurts. There was something that I depressed when I chose clarity. It was like being separated from someone, yes, from a child. It was my beloved son in my Mary-life, and now I said "away with Him." I was honest and said it already on Palm Sunday. He was torn out of me in a terrible delivery. Somewhere He had been my son and now He was to be a stranger and a lie. But I rest in myself. Under me thunders the sea. The sea is part of me like my womb or my breasts. But I rise out of the unclear and changeable wave-splash. I look out over it like a lighthouse. Clearness shines from my windows. I don't want to miss this proud consciousness. I want to die in it.

I experienced also another thing in the mass. When all the communicants had been to the altar, Englund stepped outside the altar round and knelt. He is probably too heavy to do it without support just below the altar, as the "high" do. But then it was Albert's turn. Englund turned questioning to him. *But Albert did not go out to receive.* He helped with the bread and wine, hung the little black cloth over the chalice and the paten, turned around, and sang the Thanks and the Praise and read the Benediction.

When they knelt again I saw the face. A willow twig hid His nose. There was a light that played momentarily over the forehead. I met the firm glance and said, I don't believe in You. I said it loud — I did not care if anyone heard me.

Afterwards at home, Albert asked how I felt. He looked intently into my eyes. He had understood that I had not gone forward out of any error. When I sat in the pew during communion and did not go forward, he suspected that something special had happened. But I said that I had never felt better.

He asked me why I had acted so peculiarly in the church. But
I did not want to talk about it, not yet. And I answered that
I had seen something that I wanted to see near at hand. Albert
was silent but I saw in his eyes that he had not been quieted.
He suggested that I should go and lie down, which I did not
care to do.

When he continued with his questions and his well-meaning
advice, I told him that I had seen a vision. I was furious. He
stared at me — I noticed that he was mobilizing all his
psychological terms. He looked at me as if I were a patient.
And he wondered again if I should not lie down for a while.

But I said to him that he who was a minister ought not
think that I was mad because I had had a vision. He preaches
about all kinds of people who see visions. In the gospel for the
day, Christ wept over a vision, and the whole long line —
Abraham, Jacob, Moses, Samuel, Amos, Isaiah, Ezekiel, Daniel,
Jesus, Paul, Peter, John — all had seen visions, fires and
angels, pots and almond trees, horses and chariots, lions and
eagles, rivers and cities, all kinds of unbelievable things in the
context where they had appeared. This, I said to Albert, is
what you preach about. If you remove all these men and all
these visions, there is nothing left for your religion, I said.
This is the basis for everything that you pray to God men
may eventually believe. Now a person comes and says that
she has had a vision and you answer that she is obviously ill
and you begin to think of an asylum. Tell me, in which ward
would they have put the author of the Apocalypse if he had
lived now. It is probably a good thing that he did not live in
your congregation, I said. You would have sent apostles,
prophets, and patriarchs to the asylum if they had been living
now, and yet you stand up in church and talk about being built

up in the faith on the foundation of the apostles and the prophets.

Albert said that not every vision comes from God. I answered that I didn't think he believed that any visions come from God. That is a humbug. In fact, that he doesn't believe anything of what he says.

I was sorry that he did not believe. I sensed some of the disappointment a believer feels when he is jeered at by a hostile world. I felt that my own doubt became a fraud before this ministerial skepticism. I couldn't control myself any longer. I fled up to my room.

But if he doesn't believe, why did he stay away from communion? It should have been indifferent if he took or did not take it, just so the people believed that he believed. And if he believes enough not to go to communion although not enough to take my vision seriously, the question remains, what sin does he consider committing that is so difficult to resist and so serious to our Lord that it forces him to this negative act. Our finances are pretty fair and he cannot be thinking about embezzlement. The episode with Englund he obviously considers cleared up; he cannot be possessed by such hostility that he has to refuse to go to communion with him. Is there a woman involved? I don't know who it would be. There is no one here of the beauty and intelligence required to kindle Albert's passion. Little Fröken Andersson has been fluttering about him quite a bit and looked at him with something hungry in her gray eyes, but she is too insignificant to consider.

Perhaps he is only waiting to go to communion next Thursday in Skogsby. Some ministers do not want to go to communion twice in the same week. They preach enough about communion and communion. One would think that he could not live a single day in a Christian manner without going to communion, but many of them do not go more than three or four times a year. They have to be some sort of spiritual hunger artists to believe what they preach. But they don't believe. They really don't.

I am going to break a willow branch to put in tne hand of the Christchild. It is a farewell gift, for now I know in whom I doubt. I don't have to run to church all the time to get clarity. Although this will be a difficult separation. It will be like burying Him.

It is so quiet outside. Just a little melted snow that is dropping and the tiny peep of sparrows. Otherwise it is silent. I shall go silently on the white cotton so that I shall not waken my child who sleeps in the earth. The light over the heavy snow is pale like the smile of a sick mother and the sick mother who shall die is Mary, Mary in my heart. For now I shall be Klara, and nothing else.

10

Dymmelonsdag: DAY OF SILENT BELLS*

TODAY I WENT TO DR. SKOG, A NEUROLOGIST AND PSY-
chiatrist. I also sat shaking in a crowded bus among
prattling and curious people and was squeezed into a
train where the passengers sat silent, stood silent, walked and
were silent as if they were images in a world of mirrors. I
lived in a hotel room, a mere machine to live in, impersonal
like Albert's card file, a numbered folder to keep people in.

I have submitted to this in order to find clarity. I want to
disperse all doubts that my reckoning with myself must be
taken seriously, that it is more than a sick idea. Let us admit
that in certain cases insanity can carry with it clarity in matters
a healthy person cannot penetrate, anesthetized as he is by
health's preoccupation with incidentals. But if you have a suspi-

* *Dymmelonsdayg* is the ancient Swedish name for Great Wednesday. The name derives from the practice of wrapping the clappers
of the church bells with straw on that day to ensure their silence.
The Swedish word *dymmel* may come from the English "dumb
bell," that is, silent bell. In Sweden, Holy Week was formerly
also called the quiet week. —Tr.

101

cion that you are not truly sane, a strong faith is needed to set
your own conviction against the whole world's massive and
sound thinking. Under these circumstances it is easy to reason
that perhaps I merely feel that two times two equals four; if for
Albert and for all other sound persons the answer is incon-
trovertably five, it seems more probable that they are right than
I. A certificate of sanity from Dr. Skog will simplify the
equation.

On the other hand: if I was not insane when I saw Christ
in the church, doubt has a real riddle to solve. The doubt
could be destroyed by this fact, not because the ikon is neces-
sarily a miracle but because a person who can break through
the sepulcher of my conviction that He is dead and for a moment present Himself as a reality in the present, in time and
space — such a person must have a peculiar life even though
He be dead. Or is it hyper-scrupulous to accept such reasoning?

If I am not insane, I can at least work further with the
dialectic of faith and doubt as I have lately, and Albert's compromises cannot support themselves by an appeal to common
sense. And so, I went to the doctor to get clarity. Furthermore
one ought to seek a cure when he is sick. Health is a duty
even when the sickness is clarity. I do not understand why one
must take care of one's health, but I have been brought up this
way. Ultimately this may be the reason why I have felt that
my sickness is an obstacle to my effort to arrive at clarity in
the Lenten questions.

A reception room. I sat and looked at an old copy of a
humor magazine while the church bells in the city tolled for
someone's death. I began to think about the fact that today is
Dymmelonsdag. (In the old days the clappers on the bells
were wrapped with straw on that day as if one feared that the
bells would break if someone rang them illegally.) And while

I read one humorous story after the other, I felt as if I had a fragile glass bell inwardly and would go to pieces if someone pulled on the rope. Perhaps I would not have the strength to believe. Perhaps all of this, both my Albertian compromise and my proud doubt, would be nothing but straw from a life that was a Dymmelonsdag.

It was my turn. A ceremony of greeting. A deep chair to sink into with an excellent view of a mass of instruments in a large cabinet of glass. Opposite me a gleaming mahogany table and a white coat topped by a face. The doctor looked at me with a wary look that I know so well from priests who want to provide pastoral care. The look resembles a collection bag on a stick — it hangs there in its emptiness and waits to be shown confidence.

The unpleasantness of this association, however, must not hinder me from telling everything from the beginning. This was not a question of confidences but of diagnosis. If I have a boil somewhere, it is evident that I must show it to the surgeon who is going to lance it. And I do this without thought of confidentiality. I can't understand why it should be different with psychic difficulties. So I didn't care about the confidential look of the doctor. I stated things as they were. I know enough psychology to know what I ought to say, and I talked about my being raised in a good pagan home where there was neither beating nor prudishness, only objectivity. I told of my adolescence without complications. (Sometimes I played unhappy to determine how it felt.) I told of a love affair I had when I was nineteen, quite objective and without any residual guilt feelings. And I talked of all the problems that came to me through Albert. Things I have been writing about during these weeks.

The doctor asked me if I liked Albert. What should I say?

I said that I probably did since I had been desperate about not finding him behind all his masks. That our sexual life had not been so luxuriant lately is probably the other side of my love for him. I have sacrificed the outward in order to come at the inward possibilities for a real relationship.

The next question: Did Albert agree with this reasoning? Does he agree with the effort to build up a relationship from within? I had to confess that I hadn't asked Albert.

"It isn't he who is the central figure for you," said the doctor. "You are not very much interested in him."

I said I would probably be interested if he were not so soaked in an insipid Christianity. But, I said, I have not come to get help in a marriage problem. I want to know if I am sane.

He smiled and said I probably had a drop of that dangerous poison, but not to the point where it could be called sickness. My schizoid tendency was not the real problem.

"What then is it?" I said.

"You are religiously undernourished."

"I? The minister's wife in Sjöbo?"

"Yes, you. For it is you who are religious and not your husband. But you haven't wanted to admit this. You have repressed religion like some push aside their sexuality. Your doubt is nothing more than the negative of your belief, as the sexual hate of the moralists is the reverse side of their *libido.*"

If he had suggested to me that I ought to commit adultery, it would not have angered me so much as this. He treated the question of doubt and belief as if it were a piece of psychology. The existence of God was entirely a matter of how I was inwardly constructed.

"Are you a Christian?" I asked him. He answered that he was deficient in this area. But with my temperament one ought to seriously consider if. . . .

I interrupted him. "Do you believe that God exists?" I said. And he answered that he had no competence to decide such questions. But that it would do me a great deal of good to actualize my inward piety. This he could understand, he said. If I were able to become a happy person through my faith, I ought to seek that solution and not let myself be inhibited by my intellectual puritanism.

I stared in amazement at the doctor and declared that puritanism was certainly the farthest thing from my mind.

He smiled again and said that he understood this. But my sexual paganism in the first place was not so wholehearted. Hadn't I closed the door on Albert in order to clear up what I called "important" things? Had I not denied my body its sexual satisfaction in order to be a whole person, committed, either/or, and so forth? Furthermore, he said, puritanism is probably not merely a sexual problem. The particular moral demand that it emphasizes is incidental. It is fanaticism, the demand for wholeness, the straight lines and all that which is essential. And this can probably be tolerated if one has religion, for in religion there is always the possibility of atonement for people who are so consistent that they cannot forgive themselves. But when you take God away from the puritanic, it turns into a hell.

I said that I didn't understand any of this. For if God exists, you can't get rid of Him, especially if He reveals Himself. Black must be black and white must be white, if you are a puritan or not. And if it brings about a sickness, that doesn't alter matters.

"There are many colors," he said, looking at a picture by some modern artist, a highly colored nude. The puritans were inconsistent in creating God. Now they have gotten rid of Him, though they think that He has gotten rid of Himself. If

105

we lived in a world of black and white, in a charcoal drawing or — perhaps still better — in an etching, we would probably have red dreams, and the moralists would say that they were indecent. The moralists must find every blood-red element in a world-view impossible to verify in relation to the black-and-white reality. They would probably find red and green ideas contradictory if there were someone who dared talk about green ones as well.

I looked at his white coat and thought that it must certainly be washed in a highly-advertised detergent. And his one shoe that stuck out beside the table was as black as the rest of the man was white.

But I said nothing about that. I asked him instead how he could call it moralism to try to be consistent with the truth. And he said that I could call it what I wanted to. But he for his own part could not in this connection escape thinking about the preacher from his childhood who condemned all novels because they were not true. The preacher himself had never read a book that depicted anything other than what was real or had actually happened. He was the kind of preacher who had learned that every word in the Bible was true in the same sense as an axiom from Pythagoras, and if a single word was in error, the whole Bible was humbug. It was in the same spirit that I had rejected the faith. The spirit of the puritan.

But I pointed out that no novelist presents his book as though it were a photograph of something that truly exists or has happened. It is in this area where the ministers cheat: they pretend that what they call religious truth is something more than the red and green dreams. That these truths are realities in time and space. They talk as if they had proved that God exists. They fool people into believing that they are dealing with reality and they do this by pretending that no reasonable

106

person has ever doubted or has had reason to doubt the existence of God.

There was an ironic look in his eye and he said that my husband was probably afraid to destroy the religious work of art by saying, in the midst of the novel: "In reality, this is not true." And he continued, "Is this so much worse than to behave like most of the atheists who pretend that they know that there is no God?" And he added that one ought to be honest also toward what one believes below one's conscious thoughts. If someone insists that the work of art is a photograph, I do not for that reason need to stop looking at it or refuse to open myself to it.

But I did not answer. I looked around. There was the office chair and there were all the clever office desk gadgets. Instead of the black office coat, he had the white garb of objectivity. Instead of a filing cabinet and archives, he had a glass cabinet with imposing instruments: knives, forceps, saws, catheters, drills, mirrors, all in a multitude of forms: straight, crooked, concave, convex, beautifully ordered as in a showcase for fossils.

The psychiatrist followed my glance and smiled half embarrassedly. "You are looking at my little collection of instruments," he said. "It is really a hobby; a neurologist does not need so many instruments."

He said it in such a way that my suspicions were strengthened. His tone or voice reminded me of Albert when he shows his office to a colleague: "Well, it will do. It could probably be organized a little less carefully but in such a small office. . . ." It was Albert I had in front of me. Albert in a white edition. A mystagogue inviting, initiating people into the secrets from the crypt of the soul, who wanted them to live at peace with their dreams. Therefore he wore a coat from

107

an office or a laboratory, places where reality is the only God. The prophet of the red vision collected etching pins. The man of the dim dreams sought to impress with things, with apparatus from the laboratories of a godless, dreamless world-view.

He offered me a cigarette and when I refused, he picked up an elegant cigarette lighter and. . . .

I thought if I were not mad before, I was certainly mad now. His face was double-exposed on my retina. Here was the priest, here was the doctor, and they grinned at me like Satan.

I got up and said that I didn't want to take up any more of his time with theological discussion. What did I owe him?

When I took out my twenty-five crowns to pay him, I did not dare look at the naked woman in front of him. I had a feeling that it represented me.

Albert met me when I came home. Asked me how I felt and got as an answer that I was absolutely sane. But there was something spooky about coming from the white to the black and noticing the likeness in their mannerisms: the check to see if all buttons were buttoned, the blinking into the light, their courteous way of looking at the hearer, their ingratiating voice.

I have fixed supper — I grated some dried cheese and made an omelet. We have eaten in all friendliness. The coarse linen cloth on the table; a little parsley on the butter; the old silver spoons for our tea, golden brown in bone-colored cups; quiet conversation; the circle of an evening lamp around us. Pleasant to be home again. Somewhere inside all of this, another reality: a lonely tower with closed shutters, a straw-bound bell that cannot ring, the quiet week within me that shall never end. The festival of the dead God.

It is possible that the psychiatrist is right: I am religious. This in effect corresponds pretty well with what I have arrived at before: in order to doubt, one must have a faith. Only he who is religious can achieve a legitimate denial.

Nevertheless, I do not believe that it is fear or any sort of prejudice — a kind of "puritanism" — that keeps my bells from ringing. It is just that I am nauseated by this kind of "spirituality" for which one rings the bells, this Easter that never breaks into reality but is play-acted in the "world of faith" or the "kingdom of souls." The white Albert did not try to pretend that it was a question of reality in time and space even though he clothed himself in these ideas. He remained true to his psychology. His medication had the correct label. It was, nevertheless, horrible to hear the white preacher preach. I become desperate over this prying into the "inner life." I can never let a bell ring for this kind of religion.

And so Lent continues. I shall see if I am not stronger than the Christian element within me. Doubt must conquer faith so long as the realities are on the side of doubt. For when I have elected doubt it is for the sake of truth and reality. I have chosen to keep my eyes open instead of closing them as the confessor of the inner life does when he prays. And now I know that it is not out of sickness that I have chosen this. It is to be myself.

It is Dymmelonsdag.

Such is reality. Neither Good Friday nor Easter. Gray Dymmelonsdag. It is grim; there are hellish asphalt streets in it. But Gethsemane and Golgotha exist only within. It is only within that hell makes its drama. Otherwise hell is what you find under a stone where the creeping things eat one another. This was and is and shall be. There is no Maundy Thursday and there is no Good Friday. If I could see the cross raised up out here in the church yard, perhaps Christ would break His way out of the womb of Mary and would be born. He would arise out of the grave that He has made in my psyche. And He would step out into the world of action. The word would become flesh. But Judas does not exist. Peter does not exist. Pilate does not exist. Christ does not exist. It is just Dymmelonsdag and there is straw around my hidden tones now and forever. There is no Easter Day. Christ will die in the womb of Mary. He will not rot in the grave of the inner life. I shall destroy Him slowly. Dymmelonsdag, oh, quiet week!

11

MAUNDY THURSDAY

I HAD HOPED THAT BEFORE LENT WAS OVER I WOULD BE Klara and nothing else. And I almost believe that I am. But I have a great company within me. Mary will not die. I understand that this depends upon my body that has never given birth, but I cannot be separated from my body. Perhaps it would help if I had my ovaries removed. The Bible tells us that there are eunuchs who have made themselves such for the sake of the kingdom of heaven. I would be able to do it in order to be collected in my doubt, entire and undivided, one single thing.

I understand that I ought to lead my hunger into what is Klara and get my doubt to bend down over the earth with the smile of a mother. But it can't happen. My doubt is cold and clear like the Easter moonlight out there. Mary belongs to the earth. She assumes the role of Eve and becomes mother to everything living.

She cries within me that tomorrow it will happen. He has bowed Himself before His men and He has washed their feet;

like a slave He has knelt before them with the refreshing water. He has broken bread and sung the hymn. He has gone out to Gethsemane, and now His hands crawl in the sand, the hands clench and open. There are tracks after them where they have wandered over the ground.

I am not part of this, I, Klara. It is something that aches beneath me and is played out on a shining surface outside of myself, for I am outside of it. The worst is not what happens now but what will happen tomorrow. For what will happen tomorrow is worst now. They will try Him today and a great deal of tomorrow. And then what hurts and men are afraid of will come. They will beat His back with barbed wire and lay a heavy beam on Him in order to lay Him, ultimately, on the beam, as on an operating table. He would like to ask the doctor, who bends down over Him with the hammer and the nails, if it will hurt a great deal. But He doesn't want to say this. He doesn't want to show that He is afraid of pain. No man wants to do that. And then later when the first part of the operation is over and the hands and the feet have been pierced . . . no, I don't dare think about it. But He is thinking about it now. It is always worse before the operation. I know that the theologians ignore the pain. They talk about His concern for the world and His work in the world, for Judas and Peter and us all. But Mary doesn't believe that all those nice concerns can palliate the suffering in the waiting room to Good Friday, not for the son who is God and therefore suffers with much more sensitive nerves when He is going to suffer with us. Concern for the world He has always had, but since He became man He can bleed and He has fingers that jerk and knot themselves in spasms when you put nails through the hands.

This is insanity, this also. It is a bit of faith that I cannot kill with my doubt. Not an intellectual faith, but a faith in my blood and in my nerves. That faith has grown in me like a child; like a child, and a child has its own circulation, but it is in me nevertheless and I feel how it lives.

Albert is in Skogsby for communion. I have not bothered to accompany him. I shall go the last piece of the road alone. I shall perform an abortion and then one wants to be alone. I shall abort the faith child out of me tonight and tomorrow. My hope is Good Friday. I think I shall get away from all of this when He finally dies tomorrow night. Then Mary will have no more strength.

If it is not over tomorrow night I shall take an ax and go up in the tower to kill them. In action one becomes oneself. When the pieces of wood lie in the rubbish: her crowned head, the piece of her thin, straight nose, a couple of dry logs that were a woman's torso, and a few pieces of a child; for example, a child's hand growing up out of the floor, spreading its fingers like the child's hand on the street — why shouldn't He have it like so many other children since He came to share our pain, to share our lot. When I later go down the creaking step with the ax hidden under my coat I shall have found peace in my doubt. Modern man cannot go and drag around holy mother complexes. He must be free for the facts.

Yes, I shall perform the murder. But when I think on it a little more, it seems too barbarian. People will consider it fascism. No, I shall dissolve them with my intellect. They are logically impossible. I shall write a book and execute them. That's more refined. Furthermore, the demand of truth calls me to do something to the impossibility in the church tower and in my heart. Honesty demands it.

But it will pain me. There will be pain like birth pangs. The look in the face of Mary reminiscent of insanity or ecstasy

113

— just think if that is suffering to despair. If you light her up from another direction and hold the light over her face so that her damaged chin does not destroy the image, perhaps you will see a mother who knows that she is going to lose her child very soon. There is an area where pain and blessedness meet. A little contraction in the muscles around the mouth and the smile becomes weeping. Perhaps one saw that more clearly before the paint had chipped from the face and the expression was distorted by the cracks in the wood. I must find out, for it concerns my own self. No, not myself, but a growth on my psyche that must be operated away, perhaps tomorrow.

I must make a careful diagnosis. I must do it tonight. I can't let anyone know, for it is possible that I must eventually take some very serious steps. I must be careful, very careful. I shall not go the short cut from the house to the church. No one has gone there yet today and more snow fell there this morning. I shall go through the main gate to the road and from there up to the church. No one who sees me on the road can believe that I am going there. I really ought to wait to light the candles until I have closed the shutters — if they aren't shut already — but there are so many beams on which one can strike both head and feet, and the stair down is only a hole in the floor rather treacherously placed. Hence if I don't want to risk stumbling and perhaps losing something, I should probably keep the candle lit the whole time so that I can see what I am doing. If I shield the light with something, no one can see it, at least near at hand, for the tower is fairly high. There is an old screen in the sacristy; Pastor Lindgren used in his time to urinate behind. He was very old and he had troubles of that kind. And I must take away the willow twig that I put in the hand of the child.

Now I have been in the tower. I have seen a view that I shall never forget. It surprises me that I am absolutely calm and clear. I am ice within — burning ice, but my hands are sweaty.

When I was going to close the shutters, I saw them. The car had driven away. I saw the red tail-light out on the road. There is frost damage next to the house and he probably blamed that. They came up the hill to the church. First he turned around and looked in the direction where the car had disappeared, then he put his arm around her. When they came up under the tower, they stopped. He put down the communion set, put his right hand around her waist, with a gesture I know very well, pressed her to himself, pushed back her little hat so that he could stroke her hair, just as he has done with me many, many times. It looked strange and I thought that it must be a vision, but the blood rushed to my heart and demanded that I scream or do whatever was necessary to destroy the specters under me. Then I thought of rushing down and telling them what I had seen and of showing her, the other one, the road home to Forsby. I wanted to transfix Albert and strip him of his dignity until he was only a rag in the snow. But I did nothing. He kissed her and I felt as if something in me was slowly suffocating. I couldn't move; I was like a marble statue. I stood a long time and looked at them, looked and looked.

Suddenly I remembered that I must be in the house before Albert. It would have to be he and not I who came with the explanations. And these should be postponed until I had time to think. I tore myself out of my paralysis and ran down in the white light that fell on the stairs from an aperture in the south wall, a white factual light. I hurried through the church and out through the sacristy so that they would not see me. In any event, Albert would probably think of other things

115

than my tracks when he came that way. He can come when he will. He hasn't come yet and he can come when he wishes. One thing is sure: I will not make a scene.

I want to think. First of all, it seems to me that my problem as a minister's wife is solved. I am no longer married — the divorce is only a formality that in due time will substantiate the situation. I have taken off my rings — what could bind me to Albert is dead. I notice how calmly I state this and write it down. My hand does not shake; rather it is a little stiff. I suspect that I ought to throw myself on the bed and weep and tear a handkerchief to pieces in rage. But I can see everything with cold objectivity, as if it had to do with strange people. I don't trouble myself over what he found to prefer in this teacher. That is his business; it does not concern me. And it gives me satisfaction to be able to sit here in quiet and write while he stands with her out there or perhaps follows her home to Forsby.

I now see clearly a great deal that has been puzzling during many long nights, especially that time when he was at the birthday party in Forsby and stayed late even though I was ill. Several long telephone conversations behind closed door; his readiness to follow her home so that she would avoid going alone through the woods; and his very thoroughgoing pastoral care. I also understand Albert's concern for me on my day of penance, when he would not take me sexually even though I offered him the opportunity. Apparently my intuition reacted correctly when I felt myself rejected.

Above everything else, this is the truth about Albert's "struggle," his "development," and all. He had felt himself rather certain in his faith and in his morality. Suddenly he was overwhelmed by a passion. Or was it only that he had a difficulty fasting for a long time and took his wounded self-

116

respect as a pretext for giving himself to a woman who understood him better? In any event, his safe world began to shake. He had not believed himself capable of anything like this. Perhaps he began thinking about this and that, and began even to doubt in the providence of God, which had not helped to correct him from falling. Elvira Andersson kissed him and suddenly he needed a theodicy. And he understood Peter so well. He could even consider that Pilate, Barabbas, and the common people had certain traits common to himself. Elvira Andersson came along and soon the word of God had another ring. Pastor Albert Svensson sinned — immediately the church needed a new orientation in its theology. Sooner or later he will probably construct a new section in his dogmatics involving Peter and Pilate, an additional subdivision on the doctrine of the fall.

Oh, it's the same Albert as always. The same general store with new furnishings as he needs them. That he did not go to communion on Sunday probably meant that he planned a tete-a-tete with his love. But it did not involve any risky decision. Here in the church, the people thought that he was going to Skogsby, and if he did not go to the altar there today, the people thought that he went to communion here, and in this way he could give his sermon a deeper tone of sincerity last Sunday when he talked about Judas.

The only thing that disturbs me in this story is the topic of Judas. For me, personally, Albert is a finished chapter. I am not and have never been married to anyone, for he has never been anybody. There is no fixed point in his existence. But this is Maundy Thursday. He ought to have had certain associations when he stood there kissing the woman. It was a treachery to everything he had promised to hold sacred. It is strange but his deceitfulness toward me and toward Christ

117

are the same thing. If I had surprised him naked in her bedroom, it would not have disturbed me more than to see him stand in his canonicals and kiss her. For this thought goes like an earthquake under my cold calm. It causes me to lay aside my pen to go to the window to look out, to go to the mirror, to go to the bed to shake the pillows, and to come back here again. It sends a shudder through the dead in me. It calls on the woman in me to rise up from the dead and join in the anger, to whine, scream, tear down all suns and stars. Christ, the fixed point in my negation — Christ, and I who have found salvation through doubt in Him — we together have been betrayed this night by a spiritual huckster of undetermined age, powerfully built and dressed in canonicals. And the woman was dressed in gray like the dusk and shone with understanding and admiration and Yea and Amen like gold and precious stones and pearls.

Oh, we have been betrayed on all the Maundy Thursdays and always by businessmen with apostolic credentials. In reality, perhaps, it was the same one who has betrayed us in all times, the wandering Judas who betrayed us for money or a pastorate or a woman. I hope you have put down the communion silver, Albert, so that you can hold her with both hands.

I wonder what is on the way. There are no angels walking around our house on Maundy Thursday. Here the light is clear, white, and electric. I am alone in it. I stand as if I stood on the white rock in Gethsemane. Meanwhile, what is to happen creeps closer in the darkness. It comes from without and points at our white spot. It comes closer and moves around. It looks and says, Yes, here it is. For it has not happened yet even though the communion has been distributed and Christ has been betrayed and the woman holds the apocalyptic chalice and the priest is drunk with the wine of her unchastity. Those who believe wait, that God shall break in. They say, Thy will be done. They believe that if God wills, it is now only Wednesday. But we who doubt, we know that what will happen, happens. All shall be fulfilled. No cup is allowed to pass. I don't have to hurt the Son. It is Friday tomorrow. I have no anxiety. I wait here in my circle of light to meet my destiny with a cold glance. It comes when it is ready and expects me to scream with terror when it knocks on the door and unashamedly comes in to me. But I have seen it before; I have become used to its appearance. It looks at me objectively like a doctor-executioner: now we shall do it, this is the right place to apply the instrument. It moves with the same precision as a parasite wasp when it lays its eggs in the paralyzed victim. Thus what will happen will be fulfilled. Not only from without but from within, where destiny has laid its egg in us, where the larva is hatched and eats his way to the heart. I have seen it like a monster in a painting by Hieronymus Bosch, or like a beast in the Apocalypse: the torso was like a man's and the face was like a man's; it had no arms and no legs but wings and insect legs like a wasp and the tail was a syringe. It had long hair like a woman and breasts like a woman. But have no fear of it, for what will happen will happen and I need no anaesthetic.

Yesterday he asked me if I had told the doctor about my visions. And when I told him that my visions had decided me on the question of doubt and faith, he answered that doubt and faith have nothing to do with signs and wonders but only with the forgiveness of sins. Sins against whom, forgiveness from whom? Here there is no who, there is only what. The wasp buzzes and man suspects what will happen and he screams and asks who will help, but what will happen happens. The series is fulfilled, the egg is hatched, the larva eats his way toward

119

the heart. For there is no one who can help. The series is never broken. I go toward death where'er I go.

Forgiveness of sins is the white dust on Albert's fingers when they curve around a woman's breast. He has taken this forgiveness in his right hand and he did not burn himself. Not at the altar where he distributed the bread, and not later when he met the soft, warm sin under the dress, the sin that should be forgiven. Nothing happens of what would happen if he had the forgiveness of sins on his fingers and if the forgiveness of sins were from someone outside the wasp's circle. I mean someone who will not be mocked. The earth is not shaken and no dead rise from their graves out in the churchyard. She has probably washed the blouse on which he spilled wine on Sunday so that she can have it tomorrow. It is probably not fretted by the betrayed blood. When I am gone, he will marry her and the church will affirm by the seal of God's name that their time of passion is not only forgiven but blessed so as to "lighten the burdens of life, soften its cares, through conscientious nurture prepare for the welfare of coming generations and assure the highest joy on earth, in the name of the Father and the Son and the Holy Ghost, Amen." Then they will live many happy years here in the manse. For the Lord knows His own and blessed is he who does not walk in the way of sinners. His off-spring shall live in the land, but the way of the ungodly shall perish. I wonder if they are still out there in the shadow of the church. The church tower will probably not fall over them like the tower of Siloam. And the fire of Yahweh will not burst out to destroy them. But up in the tower sits He who has the power and lifts His chubby child hand over them with two fingers in the air. He does that when He blesses.

I think of a Maundy Thursday sermon that Albert gave

in Skogsby, I believe it was last year, on Psalm 139, "If I say, 'Let only darkness cover me, and the light about me be night,' even the darkness is not dark to thee, the night is bright as the day." Albert talked about how unbelief and treachery must in the darkest of nights glorify God. In reality, the Psalm talks about how impossible it is to hide oneself from God, but Albert finds his own exegesis useful. He applies this year what he learned last year and glorifies God with Elvira under the protection of the Almighty and under the shadow of His wings. One can certainly say that this is a shining darkness.

I stop. It is as if my inner being trembled under heavy feet and I do not know who it is who wanders. The split within me is threatened by a fall somewhere in the depths. If the fissure is filled up, then night is here, and I shall lose the light of my reason. Then I shall not be able to hold apart the two realities. Then night and day will fuse in my being and Klara will become the mother of sorrows. Oh, this trembling of the underground when Christ steps down into the kingdom of death, down into Hades and Hades rises up toward the light, this pillar of cloud in the deep where the night shines as the day. If this is not stopped, the two will form a new covenant in the blood of Christ, which has been shed for the doubt that I believe in and for the faith I doubt in.

No, I must find my way back to calm analysis. I shall open the curtain to prove if I can see what actually takes place.

TRANSCRIPT

Olanda Police District
REPORT
Monday, April 20, 19—

Thursday, April 16, 19—, 11:15 p.m. A telephone message was received from the fire chief, a Mr. Lundgren of Forsby that the Sjöbo fire department had been called to the Sjöbo church where fire had broken out.

CONSTABLE NILS STROM IN FALLA, *who was ordered to report to the place, indicated that personnel from the fire department were in the churchyard when he arrived and had begun to make efforts to put out the fire. Flames had been coming from the tower and from the roof of the church and several window panes had been broken by the heat. The firemen had three hoses going but had difficulty with the water supply.*

About 11:40 p.m. the bells in the tower had fallen through two floors down into the entryway and at 12:15 a.m. the steeple burst and partially crushed the nave roof. This gave the fire in the interior of the church greater intensity. A half hour later the fire reached such dimensions that efforts had to be made to protect surrounding buildings including the parish house and the manse. At 3:00 a.m. only the stone walls remained of the church, and at 3:30 a.m. the fire department left the scene, leaving two of their numbers as a guard.

The constable had secured the services of nine reliable persons as guards. Of property of the church only a chasuble and two candlesticks of pewter were saved.

122

The church building was of stone except for the upper parts of the tower which were made of wood. The roof was covered with wooden shingles. The church had no central heating or electric light. It was heated by a stove.

The furnishings destroyed by the fire have been entered on an attached inventory.

At 8:15 a.m. on Friday, the constable found a candle holder of iron in the western part of the building.

He felt that this candle holder possibly had some connection with the cause of the fire but could not make any clear explanation. During the night the wind had been westerly.

FIRECHIEF SIMON LUNDBERG stated that KLARA SVENSSON, *the wife of* ALBERT SVENSSON, *the pastor in Sjöbo, tried to get up into the tower and returned seriously injured, whereupon she was taken to the City Hospital by her husband. This episode had taken place before the constable arrived in the area.*

With respect to the above, the following is deposed:

CHURCH WARDEN SIMON LUNDBERG, *born November* 18, 1893, *and residing at farm* 1:3, *Forsby, Sjöbo parish, received a telephone message about the fire from tenant farmer Gustaf Hansson, at* 11:10 *p.m., April* 16. *Since, according to Hansson, the fire had gotten a considerable start, Lundberg ordered the fire department to proceed immediately. The fire department reached the place at* 11:25 *p.m. and used a pump producing* 900 *liters per minute; several sections of hose had been employed, but the water in the well of the manse and of the tenant farmer had not been sufficient, and there was no other water in the vicinity. Effort to limit the fire had also been complicated by the fact that the ladders of the fire department*

123

did not reach up high enough toward the fire, which was situated in the tower. Upon the arrival of the department, the fire was localized in the tower chamber whereas the church itself was relatively undamaged.

Lundberg supported the data furnished by the constable and felt that the fire had resulted from a visit to the tower chamber during which there had been negligence with fire.

TENANT FARMER GUSTAF HANSSON, *born June 4, 1898, registered in Sjöbo parish, got up at 11:05 p.m., April 16, to look after a cow who was about to calve. He had then noticed flames in the church tower, the north shutter of which stood open. He hurried to the scene and found the church door unlocked. The stairs up to the tower were already full of smoke and Hansson could not get up to the tower chamber. He had then run out of the church to get help and had cried that the church was on fire. When he came around the north gate, he saw Pastor Albert Svensson come running up the road between the manse and the church crying, "Where is it burning, where is it burning?" whereupon Hansson answered, "In the tower." At the same time,* FROKEN ELVIRA ANDERSSON, *a school teacher, coming from the opposite direction, that is from the west gate, had run toward the pastor shouting, "Pastor, the church is burning." Hansson could not remember any other witnesses on the scene. He had hurried to his home about 100 meters from the church and called the fire chief by telephone. When he returned to the church, Fru Klara Svensson lay unconscious in the snow while her husband, Pastor Svensson, was endeavoring to cut away her clothes with a pen knife. Her dress was partly burned and her shoes were smoking. A little later, the pastor and she left by car for the city to seek medical assistance. Near the place where Fru Svensson had been lying, Hansson found a glowing piece of wood. He had kicked it around in the snow until he could take it in his hands and identify it. He thought himself able to identify it. "It was the Saviour of the world that I once saw in the church tower sitting in the Virgin Mary's lap." Hansson laid the piece of wood on the churchyard wall but has not been able to find it since.*

Hansson thought that the accident was caused by someone's negligence with fire in the tower chamber of the church. Perhaps some tramp had found the church gate unlocked and had sought night refuge in the chamber.

FROKEN ELVIRA ANDERSSON, *school teacher, born April 8, 1919, registered in Forsby school in the parish of Sjöbo, was on her way home from a service in the Skogsby church about 11:00 p.m., April 16. When she came by the church, she heard the cry that it was on fire. She hurried up to the west church gate and found Pastor Svensson running from the manse. She told him the church was on fire. While the pastor sought to make his way up into the tower, Fröken Andersson went to the sacristy to save the communion silver, especially the chalice, which is an antique and is encrusted with five precious stones. She had found the communion service in the case that was used to carry it in. The case had been standing on a table in the sacristy. Froken Andersson thought that the pastor had put the silver there since it had been used that evening at the service in Skogsby. Possibly he had forgotten the key to the chest where the valuables of the church were kept and had postponed putting away the communion service until the following day.*

When she came out of the church, Fröken Andersson saw Fru Klara Svensson rushing up into the tower, where for a

125

few moments she was discernible in the north window. Fru Svensson was working hard to tear something loose and had disappeared again. She had a dark dress and was bareheaded. When she came out of the church she had run by Fröken Andersson on her way to the manse and had been stopped by her husband. It was impossible to see how seriously she was injured. Fröken Andersson had smelled burned hair. Fröken Andersson now became nauseated and left immediately when she felt she could not be of any help.

Fröken Andersson suggested that the fire started in the tower but had no idea of its origin. She remembered the fire that resulted a year ago when a few boys had been smoking cigarettes in a straw stack and did not think it improbable that the fire in the church may have had a similar origin.

PASTOR ALBERT SVENSSON, *born November* 10, 1911, *registered in the manse of Sjöbo parish, was returning from a walk late on the evening of April 16, perhaps around* 11:00 *p.m., and had just intended to return to the house when he heard the cry from the church that the building was on fire. He went immediately from the manse to the church. He had not previously noticed any fire in the church tower. During his walk he had been completely preoccupied with his sermon for Good Friday. When he arrived at the church he met tenant farmer Gustaf Hansson. The latter, at the suggestion of the pastor, hurried home to call the fire department. Meanwhile, the pastor tried to get up into the tower from which large clouds of smoke emerged. However, he could not get through the heavy smoke in the stair. For this reason the pastor could not manage to ring the bells in the church tower and alert those who might have been of help.*

When he returned to the churchyard for a breath of fresh

air, his wife, Fru Klara Svensson, came rushing from the manse. Without hesitation she pushed into the smoke and made her way up into the tower even though the pastor sought to hinder her and cried for her to come down. After a brief minute, Fru Svensson came back. Her dress was burned and her face sooty. She held the wooden doll in her arms, a Christ image that caused her a great deal of anguish, for it was still burning. She did not want any help but sought to make her way to the manse with the doll. Even after she fell in the snow, she sought to keep her husband from taking the object from her. In his effort to take the burning object from her, the pastor's hands were blistered. Only after Fru Svensson had fainted was the pastor successful in freeing her from the object. He took her immediately to the hospital, where she died at 7:00 a.m. on Saturday, April 18. Lately she had shown evident symptoms of mental disturbance and had even sought the help of a psychiatrist. Her sickness manifested itself in an intensified interest in the Virgin Mary. Pastor Svensson felt that her interest was the cause of her rushing up into the tower and tearing loose the image of Christ from the sculpture that was preserved in the tower chamber and represented the Virgin Mary with the child.

Pastor Svensson thought that the fire had been caused by his wife. He had found some notations that indicated that Fru Svensson before the fire broke out on April 16 had gone up into the tower to study the image of Mary. The pastor would not release these notations for further investigation. He said, "These notations belong to a diary that has been given to me by my wife as a privileged communication. I cannot relinquish them. It is a matter of principle."

The pastor also recognized the candle holder that the constable found in the church's entry way. He was of the opinion that Fru Svensson in her confused state had left the burning candle in the tower, that the candle had come loose from its holder or in some other way had come in contact with shavings or something else flammable. Some rubbish had been left in the tower chamber after some repairs of a year ago.

Pastor Svensson also substantiated Elvira Andersson's account of the communion silver.

The church with its furnishings was insured in a Stockholm insurance company for 150,000 crowns and the pastor will make application to this company for the damages.

The fire insurance company had indicated that it will fulfill its commitment to Sjöbo parish but is awaiting a police report in the matter.

KLARA MARGARETA SVENSSON, NEE BORGMAN, *was born May 3, 1915, in Stora parish, the daughter of Dr. Axel Borgman and his wife Margareta Victoria, born Ogren. Klara Svensson was married to the associate pastor in Skogsby and Sjöbo parishes, Erik Albert Svensson, registered in Sjöbo parish and living in the manse. She died April 18, 19— of injuries from burns as indicated in the attached medical report.*

Olanda,

Date as above

ERIC MAGNUSSON,
POLICE ASSISTANT

Fee: 3 crowns

12

GOOD FRIDAY

Commentary on Klara Svensson's notations at the time of their being placed in the personal archives of Pastor Albert Svensson. (File B-12)

KLARA WOULD CERTAINLY HAVE INTERPRETED THIS COMmentary as a means of holding reality at a distance. Just as she thought that my love for the order and neatness in office matters was a compensation for similar tendencies in my intellectual life. I find no reason, however, to depart from my habit of providing my records with complete data, especially since I feel the need for myself to clear up some of the inexplicable episodes that are touched on in these notations.

When Klara and I were married, she was a very ordinary young lady, although of set opinions. Everything proceeded pretty well as long as she was not required to change the pattern of her life. During our first time together I was a very worldly priest, and for that reason the differences between our ideals was not so difficult to bridge. But later I was asked to serve in this parish where the parishioners do not want the minister to be like "an ordinary person," but to live and teach like a spiritually-minded man. Something had really happened in my life when I held the lecture on sexual morality about which Klara had such clearly critical opinions. I was not the same as when I fell victim to her beauty and her lax principles; the pious people in this parish had begun to exercise a deepening influence upon both my doctrine and my life. Klara resisted this influence and noted only the hypocrites she could discover in the house of the Lord. Although to begin with she seemed to be reasonably loyal, she opposed violently the change in our life pattern. When I first noticed her opposition I did not suspect that this was the first manifestation of her sickness. I should have been warned by her inconsistency, especially when at the same time she sought to embrace modern viewpoints and to defend a massive orthodoxy in preference to a more tolerant and liberal position. Not even when she began to consider herself the mother of Christ did I understand the seriousness of the situation. I was, of course, repelled by the whole matter.

Her attitude involved some very serious strain for me. I did not consider yielding to the pressure of her argument. I had seen the danger of the orthodoxy that she considered so exemplary. As assistant I had served for a time under the provost K.A.P. Johansson and had opportunity to see how an orthodox and high-churchly theology isolated the poor man from the reality that surrounded him and made him a stranger to the problems of his fellow man. But I have always wanted to be an ordinary person and was not to be led astray by Klara's contempt for common sense. It is not possible in our day to advance the opinions that she felt a minister should embrace. Furthermore, I could not betray my conviction. I have never promised to proclaim the word of God except in accordance with my reason and conscience. And the dogmas we discussed are very foreign to both.

What did cause me considerable difficulty was Klara's personal behavior. I don't think I deserved her treatment of me. She has herself confessed that I tried to be attentive to her. For many years it was my daily joy to devote myself to her. I shined her shoes and made her bed. Flowers were never lacking in her room. But I soon noticed that she was more often irritated than thankful when I tried to set things in order for her. At last I did not know how I could please her and for that reason found it best to withdraw. Naturally I also felt affronted.

This feeling was deepened by her persistent criticism and irritating questions. Not even in the presence of my parishioners did she show any respect for my experience. I understand how poor Klara was driven by her sickness to this contentiousness and could not help that time and again she put us in situations that I made endurable only through the exercise of all my skill. I understood that in these circumstances I could probably never expect promotion. I was made weary and restless in my mind by these constant investigations about what I believe and do not believe. Never a word of encouragement, much less of recognition. I have never desired admiration, but I have longed for understanding. To feel oneself watched instead of loved and never to rest in the tenderness of a woman become unendurable at last even for a saint.

When finally Klara began to deny me my matrimonial rights, I was also carnally tempted. And when I found a woman near me who wished nothing more than to give me all that I desired, I could not resist. It was a difficult trial. I know that there is forgiveness for everything — this has been the central point in my preaching. But I have never meant that one could sin presumptuously or that grace should be without fruits in the life of the Christian. Here Klara has misunderstood me. I also felt that I myself had come a distance on the road. For that reason it was a serious shock for me when I, although under very mitigating circumstances, fell for the temptation to accept the love that cried to me in the wilderness. I could not believe that I was so weak. I then began to doubt in the God who promised us that we should not be tempted beyond our ability. My sermons became either a mere formality or a recognition of the weakness of the believer. Neither seemed to give the church the edification that it had a right to expect. I tried to pray but my prayer did not go anywhere. Furthermore, it became more and more impossible for me to resist the renewed temptation.

Nevertheless, I accepted the consequences of my new situation. I denied myself sexual relations with my wife, as she herself has indicated. If I could not be faithful to Klara, I wanted to be faithful to Elvira. Furthermore, I held myself away from communion when I felt God's judgment shaking my conscience. I was honest enough not to pretend piety when I found it impossible to break my connection with Elvira. That we sought each other's company even on Maundy Thursday was consequently no treachery, as poor Klara believed. I assumed the greatest possible honesty to save what could be saved. I understood that this kind of situation could break my character and make me a spiritual cripple. I wanted to avoid the hardening that is a sin against the Holy Spirit and the consequence of which has been given in the word that whom the Lord will punish He makes blind. For that reason I let the judgment fall over myself and sought, first of all, to avoid the temptation that Pastor Johansson's example, without his knowledge, often warned me against, that is, to forget people for the sake of ideas and principles.

I understood that the situation demanded my special concern for Elvira. Only under the protection of darkness or on the pretext of official business did I visit Forsby. Not even Klara noticed anything before the last night, and her testimony can no longer hurt Elvira. I have made sure that the disturbing events that happened between Maundy Thursday and Good Friday shall not in other ways cause Elvira difficulties. When we were disturbed by the loud cries about the fire, we were on the north side of the church. But I left Elvira and ran toward the east around the church and came out on the south side, that is, on the road between the manse and the church so that it would seem that I came from home. With admirable intuition Elvira understood what she ought to do. In accounting for the origin of the fire, I have fashioned the facts in such a way that no shadow will fall on Elvira's reputation. Truth has no value in itself but must be subordinated to one's love for one's neighbor.

If I now can look to the future with a certain assurance and can in thankfulness to God feel that I have ridden out the storm, Klara's destiny is so much darker. Her sickness stamped her long before the crisis, but her notations for Maundy Thursday witness even more clearly of the injuries to her mind. Her belief that certain days ought to be specially holy so that sin is more compromising on these days than otherwise cannot be justified by evangelical theology. Furthermore, Maundy Thursday is not even a holiday among us. And even though it would be possible to imagine such a sub-evangelical idea in a normal person with a lively fancy, her sickness becomes clear in the words that I had the forgiveness of sins on my hands — this is quite simply magic. Furthermore,

I did not caress Elvira's breasts that night, which was quite natural since it was cold and my fingers were cold. The same magical illusions cling to Klara's conception that the wine I spilt on Elvira's blouse on Palm Sunday had some sort of corrosive effect.

It is true that I spilled a few drops of wine on Elvira when I met her glance over the chalice. Afterwards I was afraid that she would reject me, since she had prayed at the altar for forgiveness for what we had done. Later she thought that she had committed an unforgivable sin because we were drawn to one another and could not resist. On the evening of Maundy Thursday, I explained to her in our long conversation that at the time of the communion she had not intended to give herself to me on Tuesday. She said that when I was sure that her sin was not unforgivable, it would have to be that way, and after a time she calmed herself in my arms. Naturally I found this reliance on me very moving, especially since I never found such confidence in poor Klara. Toward the last Klara felt that if one was to believe what a priest said, it was not his personality but his office and his relation to the confession of the church that were the guarantee. Furthermore, Elvira's blouse became absolutely clean. I suggested that she take out the wine spots with a special cleanser.

I notice that the light of my memories has led me away from the question that I was about to discuss, namely, in what sense Klara was mentally disturbed. In reality, her behavior at the fire disposes of all doubt. To risk her life for the sake of a wooden doll is in and by itself meaningless. It can be unreasonable to throw yourself in the flames even when a living person is in danger, which I fortunately realized, although in despair, when Klara had rushed up into the burning tower. But it is certainly romantic, not to say melodramatic, to try to save a symbol like the Christ child. Such things happen only in sentimental narratives, a light year away from reality. Only an insane imagination can account for such an act. Klara must have been unable to differentiate between the doll and a living child that had to be cared for. She had already, as we have noted, expressly stated in her insane fantasies about the Virgin Mary that the madonna in the tower was unable properly to care for her child. This business with the Mary image was apparently an *idee fixe* with her, and I suspect that one can find cause for these sick illusions in her unsatisfied and suppressed mother instincts.

Elvira thinks that Klara ran up into the tower to try to put out the fire, and then, when she found it hopeless, sought to save what she accidentally got hold of, as people often do in fires. It happens that in their flight from the flames they will try with immense effort to take with them the most worthless thing. That Elvira wants to interpret everything for the best testifies to her goodheartedness. Certainly I also would like to believe that Klara was interested, in the first place, in preventing what she had caused and was not merely intending to save a somewhat worthless object. Unfortunately, however, I cannot share Elvira's opinion. Elvira has not been reading what Klara has been writing during these last weeks. I have not considered it advisable to disturb her with Klara's morbid brooding.

In order to get my opinion substantiated or refuted, I have written to Dr. Skog, whose services Klara sought during the last week of her life. I have asked how he could consider my wife free from insanity. The doctor answered me in a very kind manner and expressed sympathy with my great sorrow. "At the time of her visit to me," said the doctor, "Fru Svensson, as far as I could observe, was free from symptoms of psychosis, although she showed a tendency to schizophrenia. She suffered from a neurotic tension. This can be explained by the circumstances of her life and was not in itself anything abnormal." The doctor, added, however, and this is the significant thing, that unforeseen and disturbing experiences could understandably effect a radical worsening of my wife's psychic health. "But," he writes, "such experiences we should hardly expect to be common in this land of ours, particularly not in our manses."

The last word reveals, alas, a very common ignorance of the exposed position in which the clergy finds itself today. There is also something in the manner of the doctor that I do not like. It seems as if he wants to free himself from any guilt, when it is perfectly clear that he has made a faulty diagnosis. It is possible to feel a certain point directed against me in his words, but I can hardly be blamed for an accident that my wife herself has caused. I have a certain share in what has happened; no one is without sin. But the whole series of events that led to the disastrous fire was first and always determined by Klara's insanity.

To be sure, I find that Dr. Skog in his careful wording has supported my interpretation of Klara's actions on Maundy Thursday — an interpretation forced upon us by her incomprehensible thoughtlessness in leaving a burning candle in the rubbish of the tower chamber. But as I have already indicated, I cannot agree on her condition before this fatal night. I have personally experienced her fanaticism, her unhappy hyperconsistency, her painful contentiousness. These things no doctor can find, no matter how thorough his examination. Furthermore, there is her tendency to identify herself with the Virgin Mary. It is common knowledge that insane people manage to conceal their sickness when they so desire, and it surprises me that Dr. Skog remains certain that Klara was not psychotic at the time she visited him. Furthermore, as a pastor, I know a great deal about these things. Theological courses contain many books in these areas and even after my graduation I have now and then interested myself in these problems.

I would like to add that the doctor's opinion about Klara's suppressed religious need is pure nonsense. Here the doctor has approached an area that he does not understand. But that's the way it is nowadays. In other areas one has real respect for professional knowledge, but in theology everyone considers himself a doctor.

Klara's last days also testify to her confused condition. She had severe pain both on the way to the hospital and afterwards, but moaned surprisingly little. She was delirious and identified her pain with the pain of Christ on the cross, which is in itself a devotional idea. Even this loses its beauty, however, and even its plausibility when one considers her terrible burns and the purposelessness of the accident that had caused them. She seemed to follow the crucifixion with an intensity that one usually finds among people with a hysterical bent. She imagined on several occasions that she was the mother of Christ and stood at the cross so as not to leave Him alone. At times Christ was a grown man for her; at other times she thought primarily of the wooden doll that she had taken from the fire. Sometimes it was difficult to hold her in the bed and I had to ask the nurses for help. They came and held her by each arm. She then imagined that she had a cross of her own. After a while she went into a coma, undoubtedly helped by the sedation, and I was given a moment's peace to think about my beautiful church, which, as I learned later, had been destroyed by the fire. When the clock struck eleven and I could hear the bells of the city, I felt it strange to sit at a sick bed in great un-

137

certainty instead of conducting worship. After all, it was Good Friday.

When the serious mien of the doctors revealed that there was little hope for Klara's life, I came to the painful conclusion that it was probably for the best. Her schizophrenia would have embittered life for both her and me. Sooner or later she would probably have had to be taken to an asylum. Even my situation seemed simplified as I sought to adjust myself to the thought that Klara would perhaps soon go to a better land.

After twenty-four hours she opened her eyes and seemed to be absolutely clear. She talked, even though with great effort. I asked her to be quiet so that she would soon recover, but she did not hear me. "It was reality," she said, "and I could not doubt any longer. It is strange but I have had too much in common with Him to deny it. I believe in Him." Her words came in jerks and weakly, but they bore the mark of insanity, particularly the statement that "she had had too much in common with Him." The critical modern man — and she considered herself to be in this category — certainly has little in common with Jesus. Here is the same phenomenon that I noted on the day of Annunciation. It is impossible to believe that she could have come to any kind of faith. First of all, it is psychologically doubtful that a thing like this can happen suddenly for a person of Klara's skeptical tendency. In the second place, it violates all theological principles that faith can arise without repentance and guilt. Unfortunately, her confession must be seen as a manifestation of her illness. This is evident, also, from her last words, which bore the stamp of a certain levity in that she said that now the whole masquerade was at an end.

A few hours later she fell asleep. May she rest in peace until the resurrection. We shall meet again.

When I came home to my church, it had burned down. The rumor had preceded me and our tenant farmer, who stood in the church ruins on guard, expressed condolences with the deepest sympathy. The whole mood of the parish is now different than when Klara lived. Everyone understands that Klara's peculiar actions resulted from her insanity and did not originate with me. Even Mr. Alm has shown me great kindness. And when at a recent meeting of the church council the question was discussed whether the manse should be repaired — of course, the problem of the new church building must first of all be solved — a couple of the members of the council indicated that since there would soon be an election for rector in Skogsby, the question of the repairs of the manse would probably be reconsidered at that time. Thus, even an accident can contribute to the fulfillment of the promise that for those who love God, everything works for the best.

The doubts that for a time shook me have given way. I feel as if I have been cleansed and purified in the fire of testing. It is no longer difficult to believe in the forgiveness of sins and the grace that is new every morning. "God gives fortune to the honest."

Elvira has shown me the greatest understanding and shared my deep sorrow with me. This has been evidence for me of God's grace and mercy, and I have been able to apply the words of the hymn that even I "after a bitter Good Friday may await my Easter morn."

This is the hymn that I quoted in Klara's death notice. It will also be inscribed on the gravestone of black granite that I have ordered for 500 crowns at Svensson & Lindblom. Poor Klara will have a beautiful grave.

Sometimes I feel lonely among the things that remind me of Klara. If I come into the vestibule, I see her clothes hanger empty. (I gave her fur coat to my mother.) If I come into the dining room, I see her sitting there as during the tasteful dinner that she arranged for Englunds, a bit quiet and shy, a slight flush on her cheeks, and leaving the entertainment to me. If I go into the office, I see all the instruments of my responsible work that were so often the object of our small verbal dueling. If I go up to the bedroom, I see the mirror she smashed. It is now being repaired, for when Elvira saw how badly damaged it was, she advised me to get it repaired. There seems to be a shortage of this sort of glass and the stock may be depleted. Everywhere I have these memories. But I comfort myself with the words of the hymn, "Our time of sorrow shall pass away, but not thy peace."

I shall now seal this book together with the police report of the disastrous night and place the notations in my private archives. I think of the day when the books shall be opened and all secrets shall be revealed, but I am fully convinced that God shall be gracious to poor Klara. No one shall be judged by a light he did not receive, and it is well to believe and to hope that there was much behind Klara's confused mind, much that shall flower in that world where there is neither sickness nor pain.

When I now put this book in the large dresser where I keep so many personal mementos, I feel as if I were preparing to lower a casket into the grave. I close with the words from our burial ritual for children:

> *The Lord gave, and the Lord took away,*
> *Blessed be the name of the Lord.*

A Note on Olov Hartman

The name of Olov Hartman first registered in my consciousness at an outdoor performance of his play *Den heliga staden* (*The Holy City*) in Sigtuna in 1953. Sigtuna is an idyll. It is tucked into an inlet of Lake Mälar, and although only a few kilometers from Stockholm, is remote, sleepy, and wonderful. Hartman's play was about Sigtuna and not Jerusalem, for in the eleventh century the former was Christ's first town in Sweden and it reared its gray stone bell towers in defiance of the heathendom around it. At the literal level Hartman's play is a dramatization of the life and death struggle between Thor and the White Christ in the narrow lanes of the holy city. At the symbolic level it is an interpretation of the battle between spiritual and secular values that presently rages in the world far beyond Sigtuna.

Hartman's talent for finding a dramatic kernel in the husk of ordinary existence is manifested also in *Holy Masquerade,* where the stuff is drawn from a vicarage in rural Sweden. Normally the life in a country manse would seem too mousy to admit drama, but Hartman breaks through the respectable façade and finds both atheism and a kind of murder. Here also the particulars, while retaining their concreteness and plausibility, rise above mere parochialism into universality. The war in the manse at Sjöbo is fought on all the fronts of the world.

When Hartman is not creating such characters and situations, he serves as pastor in the national church of Sweden and as the director of an educational and cultural foundation under Christian auspices called *Sigtunastiftelsen.* Born in 1906 of parents active in the

141

Swedish Salvation Army, Hartman returned to the older church and was ordained into its clergy in 1932. It has been said that the Hartmanesque flair for the intense and the dramatic is a heritage from the crimson flags and snarling trumpets of the Salvation Army. But whatever their origin, the Hartman blood and fire are evident in all he writes. He believes that Christianity matters and that the treasures in tradition and rite that the church has amassed through the long centuries glow with meaning. But the meaning is not aesthetic or even priestly; the matter and the meaning are Jesus Christ and Him crucified. It is of Him and His body that *Holy Masquerade* speaks.

— KARL A. OLSSON